Also by Daniel Frearson

Dearest

The Athereon: 1

The Athereon: Day of Reunion

The Athereon: Midnight

The Athereon: Era of Man

The Last Dragon Slayer

The Doll

67-49: Classified

Clarification

Rose, Jo, *the husband* and any other characters mentioned in or referred to during this book do not exist. They are not real people. I do not know them or their lives. They are a product of my own imagination.

Any resemblance they may have to any reader or someone you may know is purely coincidence.

This book is a work of fiction purposed for the enjoyment and entertainment of you, the reader. Nothing more.

Dearest Rose: Letter's Lost

Dearest Rose Letter's Lost
ISBN-13: 9781797760070

Note

Whilst faithful to the original, this is not a direct sequel or prequel to the book Dearest Rose. Regardless of this fact it can also not be referred to as a spinoff either. This book does cover a lot of the same bases as the original did and as such was imaginatively challenging to write.

I suppose what I am saying is that this book only exists as a stop gap. To quieten down those who remind me time and time again that I left large amounts of the story blank or up to the reader's imagination.

This book exists only to cover the areas of the original story that my now improved and matured writing style and raised confidence and dedication would have allowed me to add in had I written Dearest Rose as I am now.

This will not answer all of your questions and it will not provide some revelation as to the cliff-hanger of an ending that existed in the original book.

Additionally, this will be my last voyage into the Dearest Rose story. There wouldn't be much point in returning except to do exactly what this book was meant to do all over again. There is nothing more to write past this point. The story is now over.

I only hope that after reading this, you will still enjoy it all the same. I certainly enjoyed the change of tone compared to my usual work.

Daniel Frearson

LETTER

1

Dearest Rose

It is with the unfathomably deep depression that is the bottomless chasm of my own unwavering regret that today of all days I write this fabled letter to you. My one true love.

Just look at me now.

The state that I am in.

I'm sat here barely even able to keep my tears from dripping on the page whilst I slouch in my old leather chair here at home, holding a pen in my shaking hand and carefully jotting down each word. I'm here, in the home that we picked out, remodelled and decorated together, in the office chair that you surprised me with just a day after my previous one had broken almost three years ago now, taking my time with my heavy and broken heart to write this letter because I've found myself unable to stop thinking about you.

And I doubt that I ever will.

And on today of all days, the one day in all of time that could have been seen as the least appropriate to do such a thing – the day of your funeral – I have seen it fit to begin such a saddening act as to write to you once again. To attempt to reach out my hand and the shattered pieces of my heart to you Rose. To grasp for the love and warmth that you used to bring me and to in some way, be able to communicate with you. Wherever you might be now.

To seek out and o contact my dearly departed wife.

My only true friend in life.

And my partner. In every sense of the word.

It has been forty eight days now. Forty eight harrowing sets of twenty four hours passages where I have felt completely and utterly abandoned by you my love. However, with that harsh and almost cruel sense of blame stated on paper, I want you to know that I do not hold you responsible for what happened in the end. Honestly, that much will always remain true,

Because it wasn't your fault.

If I were superstitious or religious perhaps I might have blamed god or fate for the unbefitting punishment I received when the world took you away from me but I am not such a man. You know me as such. My decisions are based in logic and based heavily on my anger also.

Yes losing you has broken me, more so than I might actually be capable of putting into words, and though my friends and family may one day see this letter and any more like it as obvious signs of a man whom has chosen not to let go of his lost past, I myself see it as my only way forward.

And I would hope that you might agree.

I cannot live without you here with me Rose. I haven't known any other such life in over a decade. I don't even know what my existence was like before I met you now. My memories of this have already been replaced. By you.

I'm not sure that I can cope on my own.

You and I both know this much to be true.

But no matter my reservations or fears, my own limitations, I have to ignore them all. I have to push past them as though they weren't even there. Because I made you a promise not too long ago now and I intended to keep it then and I still do now.

Ultimately it was your decision to make in the end. It was your body. But it was our miracle, one that I helped to make, that would eventually cost you your life. Nor myself nor you alone are responsible for this. The blame is shared in that regard.

You see, it wasn't god. It wasn't cosmic fate. And it wasn't any other manifestation of evil or malice that took you from me. And if I'm being completely honest, it wasn't down to us either.

It was just bad luck that you were born that way and it was even more unfortunate that the one thing that would eventually take you from me was a decision that was meant to bring us closer together.

As a family.

I knew that what we did would one day cost you your life. Not just that it could but that it would. I knew that there was no certain way of avoiding it forever. It would just be there, in the background of our lives until it struck. I knew that part. And for what little it was worth back then I did try to accept that fact.

But we never expected it to be this soon.

Those short few months were nowhere near enough.

We deserved more.

You deserved more.

Your mother whom you said had suffered the same fate lasted until you were five in the end. Enough time for you to have gone through a large portion of your childhood with her. Enough time to have met her and gotten to know her. And I had hoped that at the very least we would have had a similar length of time.

But not even half a year down the line and you took a turn for the worst almost overnight. Then before I truly knew it in my heart, you were just gone. And I couldn't do anything about it. We didn't even get to say goodbye.

Well, you didn't.

I on the other hand did try.

But you stopped me, remember?

You said that you would make it through this, that you would fight on and save your words for another day. But you never did get that chance.

Oh how I wish. Oh how I pray.

That if given the chance to go back and do it all over, to speak with you just one more time even if just for a moment, that I would be given the opportunity to hear you say those words Rose.

Even if you weren't ready to say goodbye, just hearing you say such a thing to me, to be able to acknowledge that there in that moment you were never going to come back, then I might have been able to bring myself to accept your untimely passing a little easier than I have done thus far.

For as current, I am yet to say the words.

Writing them down on paper like this, knowing that no living soul is ever going to actually read them, makes it almost seem like a dream. Some trick of the mind or hallucination. Some hypnosis. It just doesn't seem real yet.

I am not denying it.

I know that you are dead. Taken from me forever.

But I have found myself just sitting here at home waiting for you to get back from work like I always have. Nothing has changed in that regard. In fact I almost fear the point in the oncoming future where it will.

I never wanted you to go Rose.

In fact if given the choice I would join you.

But I must ask that you do not fear for me even as I say such things Rose. I ask that you do please try not to worry over me and the state of my mind now that you are gone.

Because we'll cope. Someway and somehow. I'll manage.

I promised you that I would.

For even in the utter abyssal darkness of your absence, I can clearly see a light even now. Our daughter, our little Jo; she will miss you, I am sure of it. As you can imagine, so too will I but the fact of the matter is, that I want you to know that we will be fine on our own.

We may encounter difficulty, speedbumps, potholes; but we will make it through. Alive, kicking and healthy. Happy. That was the promise. To raise our daughter in the exact way that we would have done together. With all the love, care and affection that she would ever need. In complete safety. Never knowing true pain or despair and always knowing that her parents are there to watch over her.

That was how you wanted her to be raised and if I can give her even half of everything that you alone would have, then it should be more than possible to achieve this on my own. Because after all, you were going to smother her with more love than she could handle as she got older. Weren't you?

I could just see it. A slight shimmer in your eyes whenever you stared at her. And I recognised it. Because it was the same way that you used to look at me.

She may never get to grow up with a mother that she can talk to, laugh beside and play with until the dark of dusk and the morning light of dawn and I may never become anything more than a single parent working from home to spend as much time with her as possible but without you here with me, even though it hurts, even though I would wish for anything else, I believe that I can handle it.

Because as long as I make sure that she still grows up knowing about you. Learning about you in every way. Getting to know you even if you aren't here to show her yourself. I know that she'll turn out just fine.

In fact I'll make sure of it for it.

Even though you will no longer be capable of doing it yourself I will make sure that she gets to know all about you just like I did. To know your high pitched childish laugh, your sweet and subtle smile, your soft peachy face and your kind heart. I will imprint them all into her. I know that I will.

I just don't know how quite yet.

But she is just one little girl after all, how difficult can it be to watch over and teach her?

Look at me. I almost sound confident.

That would be the day.

But in truth, I only this question honestly. And that is only because, you were the one who said you would walk me through it when she was born. I honestly have no clue how to look after a child, especially on my own. But it is my responsibility now. And I will rise up to the challenge with every bit of strength, courage and insight that I have. You have my word on that.

But I do still wonder. Of course I imagine it at least. The idea of you being out there somewhere somehow. So that's why I have to ask. Are you up there somewhere, in the clouds even now, watching me with your big brown eyes as I write this?

And if you are, are you at peace? Are you happy? Are you safe?

I have to wonder if you can even feel such things anymore. Do human emotions even still count for anything now?

I wonder if you can even hear me as I talk to you each night as well.

I wonder, what is it like for you now? What can you see, what can you hear? What do you think? Are you somewhere nice, somewhere where you feel protected?

I wonder now if... if I will ever see you up there Rose. Will you be there? Amongst the stars shining in the night sky, waiting for me? And I have to wonder if your mother is up there somewhere too.

Whilst it might have been a disease that took you from me in life, I assure you, it will take far more than that to keep me from you in death. I know it.

I had promised you that I would always be there, to be by your side and to protect you no matter what you faced but in the end when your time of need finally arrived, I only failed you. The disease that you contracted – complications from childbirth associated with your bloodline – modern science, medicine and myself could do nothing to stop its progression.

We both knew that having a natural birth would endanger you long before you even got pregnant, I just didn't know that the danger would be so quick to become so severe. For a mere ailment to have taken you from me just like that, it fills my heart with dread and regret.

For not anticipating that such an outcome would come up out of nowhere without signs. I regret not realising that the choice we made together and the decisions that I in part made, the actions that I took, would in some small way force me to take your life from us both.

I regret not being able to talk you out of it.

I regret not saving you.

But you had always wanted to be a mother hadn't you?

Even when we met as simple teenagers, innocent of adult life and responsibility. Of parenthood. You had already decided that you wanted a child. Even though you already knew the risks.

In that way Rose, I suppose that you were born ready for it.

No amount of puppies or kittens could have satisfied you, no amount of distraction either. You needed a child to feel satisfied with life and in giving you one, I took that life away and ended it.

We weren't even trying for a child at the time were we? It was just by merest chance that it happened. I don't know if it was my fault or yours but obviously our attempts of preventing pregnancy unless we were both sure had failed hadn't they?

I wonder, did you secretly plan for this to happen?

Was it your choice to conceive or was it truly an accident as you swore it was?

For not only a condom to have failed but also your pill, leaves me with doubt. Questions. I can see only two possibilities here now. That either the astronomically unlikely chance of both contraceptives failing at once occurred or it was no chance at all.

I do not intend to put any blame on you, to speak ill of the dead, but I do believe that you chose to do this. I believe that you chose to become a mother and simply never told me about it.

And I believe with how well I knew you, that I should have seen something like this coming years ago.

But I didn't foresee this outcome and dwelling on the past is never going to allow me to move onward towards the future in your absence. So I promise you this. If it was you, then I will find some way to forgive you in time. And if it wasn't you, then I pray that you will one day come to forgive me.

You must understand, I grieve your departure from this world. And grief is a very dangerous emotion indeed. It makes people say things, do things and think things that they would have never done normally and in my case, I fear that my mind is desperately trying to find someone to point the finger towards and with you already gone, I believe that I am now beginning to blame myself more than I know you ever would.

I do not know what more to say to you now though Rose. Your coffin was buried hours before I started writing this, so long ago in fact that the picture of your casket being lowered into the ground is already beginning to cloud.

I think that it would be best for me to rest for a while. To clear my head. Don't you?

I wish you the best on your new journey though Rose. Know that I will think of you always, and that both myself and Jo will have you in our hearts forever from this point on.

Know that I will always love you my dear, know that I will never forget you and know that although this is a goodbye, it is by no means a farewell.

I will find you one of these days, that is yet another of my promises to you my love. But for now I must go. I must go and see to our darling daughter.

So I promise to write to you whenever I can from now on. So allow yourself to rest easy knowing that the next letter is always just around the corner and don't you ever believe that I would abandon you.

Because I love you.

My dearest Rose.

2

Dearest Rose

I have found myself thinking back on this often as of late. I suppose in some small way, now that you're not here beside me, reminiscing on such things helps me find a slight sense of peace at night when I tirelessly attempt to avoid my thoughts of dread whilst I drift off to sleep alone.

But as you are obviously aware, I have never been a master of the mind or heart. Either my own or yours. So my own opinion on why such thoughts are going through my head each night is hardly one that should be taken as scientific fact.

However, no matter what reason it is that I have been revisiting these times recently, I am simply glad that I can still remember them so clearly.

Because when I sit up at night, staring into the dancing tree branches in the shadows on the bedroom ceiling, feeling the cold emptiness of your pillow sat next to me and listening to the gentle breeze of the countryside just on the other side of our walls through the crack in the frame of our window that I never got around to fixing; I think of this and every time I can't help but brandish a smile upon my face.

Thinking of you could never do anything but bring me joy.

Even with you gone this remains the same.

No matter how much your pictures around the house remind

me that you're not here. No matter how much Jo cries out for you each night. And no matter how many times I hear that our friends and family are sorry for my loss. I can only look back on the times that we spent together and laugh.

Viewing them as the happiest years of my life. The most fulfilling and most important years that I ever expect to experience. And thinking back on them, thinking about you, whilst it pains me deeply to know that you will never hold my hand again and never get to laugh at my terrible jokes or try to poison me with your cooking; when I'm thinking about you – the person you were and beauty that you held – I can only smile.

I don't know what I ever did to deserve a woman like you. I really don't.

I cannot fathom what random act in my life had granted me the favour of whatever deity it was who gifted me the chance to meet you, to know you and to love you. But whatever it was that caused this and whoever they are, I thank them greatly for allowing this to happen.

You know full well that I am not a religious man. I never have been. So understand when I say that if it was a god that brought the two of us together, some form of destiny, then I would gladly accept that as fact in a heartbeat.

Because you were the kind of woman, the absolute imagine of perfection in my life, that I never dreamt of having. You were the one thing that I never expected to find.

My everything.

That was what you were.

I'm sure that I've told you that at least a few times before. Perhaps more than even that. Do you remember?

You laughed, shrugged it off as though I were kidding. Tried to explain that you weren't special in any way and I had to interrupt you to stop you from lowering yourself too far past the point that you had already reached.

Because you truly were an exceptional woman Rose.

Gifted in art and literature. Well versed in world history and economics. And you were funny. You were smart. You were beautiful. You were... perfect.

A muse in a human body.

A goddess, walking the earth.

My light that could shine through any darkness.

And my one true love.

Do you remember the way that you looked at me in the mornings when you first woke up and then again at night when we would share that one last kiss before going to sleep?

I do. I can picture it even now. In perfect clarity.

And whenever I picture it, whenever I remember seeing it in person, I recall how it made me feel. The sensation that it caused. It was something that even now as I wrote this a month after your passing and years after I first experienced it; that I cannot adequately put into words. In fact I doubt that I even understand it myself.

This feeling was like a sense of reason, belonging and compassion mixed into one unbelievably powerful emotion of attraction. A sense that you, sitting next to me each morning and each night, looking at me like that, was my sole reason for living.

Just seeing it again would bring me such joy now.

But I am not a greedy man.

I had more than enough of a chance to memorise that imagine. So much so that I managed to do just that a long time ago.

In fact, I'm so lacking in greed that I struggle to recall a time when I had ever actually wanted for anything physical. I don't believe that it ever happened.

I never wanted anything.

Save perhaps, for you.

From the moment that I fell in love with you, you were everything that I desired and craved in life. Everything that I wanted to be and everything that I wanted to achieve. Every goal I had from then on, revolved around you and you alone.

I wanted to be your husband, standing by your side for better or for worst until the end of time. And I wanted to achieve what I had believed to be impossible.

I wanted to win your heart.

And if you remember correctly. Though I stumbled and fell more times that I could count, even though I failed time and time again to properly woo you. You still said yes.

Didn't you?

What I have been thinking about recently. What I have been debating within my mind over and over each time the sun goes down. Is whether or not your decision to finally go on a proper date with me past the small exchanges of words and signals whenever we would pass in town, was out of pity.

I do not mean to accuse you of anything Rose. You know that I would never even think of such a thing. However no one is infallible. And no matter what my own view of you might have been, no one is perfect.

From all my advances and attempts back then I would have understood and still might have now if your acceptance of my offer had been out of pity for me but I can't be sure.

So my question to you now my love. My one inquiry.

Is for you to tell me how it was exactly that the two of us wound up together like we did.

If the dates in my memory are correct, the anniversary of our meeting came to pass recently. I'm not entirely sure why I have managed to remember this small piece of information when I can scarcely remember to buy milk when you used to ask but there was something about that day wasn't there?

Some alignment of the stars that pulled us together like that.

In fact now that I think back on it, there really is no other way to describe what happened then is there? Our meeting that day was nothing short of destiny.

We were both so young at the time, barely even into our teens when our paths first intertwined and even though we hadn't yet met face to face, even though we hadn't yet spoken our names or even hear each other's voices, what we did back then shaped our futures permanently.

For one day, one rainy day in the middle of a gloomy summer, you lost something precious to you, didn't you? A locket, buried in the dirt not too far from the circus ground that you had visited earlier that fabled night.

You looked for hours. Screaming at everyone around you to help but none but your father even bated an eyelid. And though he himself did try, neither you nor he could see it amidst the crowd and the much.

You never thought that you were going to get the chance to see that locket again did you? You had thought it lost forever. Went home crying your eyes out and feeling so ashamed to have been so careless with something that important to you.

It was the locket that your mother had left to you before her passing if I recall. I would open it now to look but your jewellery collection is so large and varied, finding it could take me a day. And I would like it if I could do my best not to disturb your things if I can avoid it. Especially your clothes.

The less I do, the less likely I am to think back on the last time I saw you wearing each one of them.

Back to the point. Your mother who was taken from life the same way that you would later be had gotten a chance that you never did didn't she? She got to raise her daughter. For however short an amount of time it might have been,

And when the time came, when she knew that she was going to die and that no one could do anything more about it, she didn't say goodbye with words did she?

Instead she took your hands, placed that locket and its chain into them and closed your fist tightly around it. Told you to always look after it. To hold it close to your heart because a piece of hers was contained within.

You might have been too young to understand what she was actually telling you at the time but you took her words to heart and cared for that locket as though it were a piece of her. Perhaps in your eye it actually was.

I can remember how much I liked hearing this story when you explained it to me. It was so simple a thing to do but so special as well. Passing an item from mother to daughter like that on her death bed. I don't know why but I always admired it.

I believe that you were intending to pass it down to Jo one day weren't you? Either way, when the time comes for her to learn about you, when it comes time to answer every question that I know she is going to have, I will make sure that she gets it.

And I will be sure then, to tell her the story behind it. The miracle of our meeting that its existence helped to bring about. And I will tell her, that like your mother, a piece of your heart is contained inside. Because it is. Isn't it?

In all the commotion of that night as well as your confused feelings brought about by puberty and the situation unfolding around you with your father, you had taken it off from around your neck to stare down at it as you often did when you were feeling afraid. And when bumped to the side by a passer-by just moments before being pulled back to his side by your father, you dropped it unintentionally amidst the chaos of that moment.

It was during this time; whilst you, your father and his new found girlfriend paid a visit to that circus, feeling fear from the changing landscape of your father's love life, you had looked to that locket to calm yourself. And as a result, it was taken from your hands and quickly wound up in mine.

I had been searching for something else at the time, a discarded piece of paper from what I recall, the missing piece to a note that had been left to me.

One that I never found.

But whilst searching for it in the mud of that empty street I came across your locket as it shimmered in the dusk lit sun. The face of the small child and stunningly beautiful woman inside were mesmerising to me as I saw them. And then on the back of it, engraved for all eternity, was the name of your grandmother and your own as well.

Rose.

But I knew nothing about you then, nothing other than how you had once looked as a toddler and how your mother had looked not too long before her illness had set in.

But even so, looking at those images each night as the young man I was often made me wonder. What kind of a person were you? Where did you live? Had we ever met, even in passing?

And would our paths ever cross again?

I would think about that a lot back then.

I would dream about it too.

And through luck or destiny, that dream came true one day didn't it Rose?

Because I did find you didn't I?

And in turn, you saved me.

I don't know how my life would have played out without you in it and that locket was the reason that I never got forced down that road. I am so glad that I never had to find out what a life without you would have been like. I can think of no crueller hell.

I do hope that you are still thinking of me as much as I am of you.

And as always, even if it's just for the sake of my weakened sanity and my long standing tradition whenever we spent time apart; I will write to you again soon my love.

My dearest Rose.

LETTER

3

Dearest Rose

Of all the things to hold me up in both thought and day to day life, I would have never expected this to happen.

You see, I have found myself at an impasse of sorts in recent days my love. Perhaps it has been longer. I don't even remember that part now.

The reason I tell you of all people, is because I am struggling to bring myself to believe that this is one that I will be capable of working through on my own anymore. Not given what it's about.

It's the crying Rose. Both my own tears and snivels as well as our darling daughter Jo's. They've stopped now.

I still mourn your passing, That much is unlikely to pass any time soon. I still grow sad over my loss but I can no longer bring myself to tears over it.

I'm not even sure why.

Our daughter, Jo, she... she's gotten so big you wouldn't believe it. I can hardly recognise her. I know that children grow up fast at her age but I never expected the sudden changes that I am seeing now.

She's even managed to waddle her first few steps today. I suppose that out of everything else, every other minor detail and thought that I had wished to convey to you today, this would be the thing that actually brought me to decide to write to you once again.

It's only been six weeks since you passed.

Just six.

Jo's barely even six months old and yet she laughs at my jokes and those finger puppets you bought for her like a champ. She's curious about everything around her in the house and every noise that I make - honestly it can be a little difficult to set her down in the evenings if she can still hear that I'm awake in the next room.

And she's so smart.

Her weight is going up in equal proportions to her size as well you should know. Forcing me to feed her more and more with every serving as she demands more and more food to fill her insatiable appetite.

And don't even get me started on clothes.

I've had to completely replace her wardrobe twice since you passed and expect to do it again before she's one. Even if I buy clothes that I designed to stretch, they won't last long enough to make a difference.

I guess that I'm just going to have to get used to it. She'll do this a lot as she gets older. Every child does but girls especially. Playing dress up is just a part of their DNA I suppose.

She was already starting to show signs of crawling before your illness progressed wasn't she Rose? Well even if she wasn't and I'm remembering events out of order once again, it didn't take her a lot longer to figure out the rest of it.

She's still small enough that she can get behind the cabinets and chairs to hide from me if I take my eyes off of her for even a handful of seconds, so watching her is becoming a constant challenge as she becomes faster and more mobile.

Thankfully she hasn't quite mastered her balance or the act of walking, she is only six months old after all. If she was that developed already then I would be equal parts impressed and worried. Because I probably wouldn't be able to keep up with her.

As for the rest of her developments though, she is yet to make any more significant milestones than those that I have already mentioned.

But she has plenty of time left.

Even for the brightest of children, communication in any form at the age of six months would be exceptionally rare. And we can hardly be expecting her to know how to read yet either.

But I am looking forward to everything that is to come in her life more and more as each new day presents itself.

It must have been so challenging for her Rose. To adjust to her new life with me as a single father.

God, even writing that on paper feels wrong.

But in just these six weeks, I have seen her grow so much emotionally that you wouldn't believe it.

She's less fussy when it comes time for her feeding or changing and she's a much quieter sleeper than I can recall her ever being before or after your death.

As I mentioned she has finally stopped her crying. In fact she barely even gives me a peep when she's scared or sad. She just goes stiff and stares.

I wonder if I am to blame for that.

You understand that on those nights when she would cry as loudly as she could as though her lungs were going to burst I had no choice but to just let her ware herself out.

I couldn't give her any comfort. Not when it was you that she was crying over every time.

I don't believe that her brain can in any way process the loss of her mother at such a young age but in some minor way, she is aware of your absence. And that alone was enough to make her cry.

I am saddened deeply knowing that she had to go through that and even more so when I tell myself that she has finally learned to accept it. A child that age shouldn't be brought to tears like that. And a child her age shouldn't have to grow up without a mother.

It just isn't right.

The impasse that I have found myself at now is questioning what I should do with myself next.

If I can no longer bring myself to tears over you and our daughter cannot do the same. If the worst of the emotions have passed and the rest is to remain internal and hidden for the both of us. Then what next?

I try to keep myself busy as much as I can.

I bury my head into work at any opportunity I get, even managing to get more done that I ever did before I lost you but that still isn't enough to take my mind off of the subject.

I know in my heart that you are never going to walk back through that door and come running into my arms as you would every day after a long shift at work. And it's tearing me apart.

To sit here every day, in the house that we picked out from the dozens of others in our price range and lived in together for over a decade. To be surrounded by so much of the furniture that you picked out either with me or for me in every room and every memory that they invoke when I look at them. I am struggling to admit that it might be too much for me to bear.

But we both know that I am not one to repeat myself.

Especially not to you Rose.

You always did your best to listen to every word that I had to say and always took it to heart. You even remembered what I had told you better than I did half the time. And I loved you just that little bit more because of it.

So when I tell you now that loosing you has been hard on me, you already know why. Because I've already said it all to you before.

When I look to the future now, I don't think that I will ever be capable of moving on. Not fully. But I do expect that I will be able to bring myself to come to terms with the loss that I have faced. However I have no clue as to how I am to do such a thing just yet.

But I guess I've still got time to work on it.

Speaking of work, I've been keeping myself busy outside of caring for Jo and my job if you can imagine it.

Just think, your lazy slob of a husband who only got off his arse to work or to do as he was asked or told actually showing some initiative and getting things done on his own. I can barely believe it.

But it's true.

I've patched up the fence panels in the southern flower garden, I've mowed the front lawn, organised the gardening and the tool shed's, fixed our bedroom window and even put a fresh coat of stain over the floor in our dining room. And that was just what I did this past week.

Going back further than that, well, the list goes on.

Spring seems to be getting warmer now though, so summer will start soon. Which means I'll only be encouraged to even more than I am doing already. You know how much I enjoyed a good bit of sun.

Though, it's still not as warm as either of us would have liked it yet.

I can hardly call twelve degrees warm. But it's better than nothing I guess.

I still haven't seen that goose though. The one that used to visit the pond across from the flower garden over the hill every year around this time. I do hope that it hasn't died of age or been eaten yet. It was always so friendly and never once tried to eat the fish or bite at our hands.

Though, I'm not entirely sure that it would eat the fish anyway. I don't know that much about geese. They could be herbivores for all I remember from school. I never was one for biology.

Academics in general really but the sciences even more.

However, other than all of that Rose, I'm not sure as to what else I have to cover now.

If I recall, I mentioned your locket when I last wrote didn't I?

How it had been the guiding thread that had pulled us together.

Well I think I finally remembered.

Not that I had actually forgotten.

But looking back on it now, I believe that I can now recall every little detail of its story.

However, I'm afraid that it's getting a bit late for any of that now.

The only time that I can find to write these letters to you is always in the middle of the night when Jo has been set down, the staff have gone home and I have no more work left to finish.

So I will do my best to write to you again in the morning should I get the chance. I would hate to leave you hanging like that forever.

Please wait for me until then.

You'll hear from me soon.

My Dearest Rose.

4

Dearest Rose

It is so odd, so unnatural, for me to have to start my letters to you now without first asking you how you are and what you've been up to.

It's almost wrong.

A conversation is meant to go two ways. Give and take. Send and receive. But now, no matter how much I write or how many questions I ask of you, I know that I will never get a reply.

You can't tell me how you have been anymore. You can't even tell me what you've been up to. And that almost breaks my heart to think about. Because those tiny little pieces of information, were the highlight of my day in the past.

Whenever we would spend time apart, even if it were just for a few days, we would write to each other to pass the time. Impatiently awaiting the next letter to arrive with every passing day. Anticipating what small amount of humour or compassion they might have contained as though we needed them to survive.

And though I used to try my best to avoid any part of my job that would have taken me away from you and you too tried to do the same, I realise now that it happened so often regardless of our efforts that there might not have been much point in trying in the first place.

But I am serious Rose. I used to love getting your letters. About as much as you used to enjoy receiving mine. And I suppose the most difficult part about writing to you now, the most challenging truth to accept, is that I will never get one of yours. I will miss them almost as much as I miss you.

I miss your hair, your face, your sense of fashion. Your strawberry lipstick, your perfectly round brown eyes that shimmered even in the dimmest of lights and your smile. Your short and sweet smile. Able to lighten up any room. The slightest of curls on both your lips and the smallest hint of them trembling whenever they moved.

Never showing your teeth, always closed and yet, never truly shut. I would wager as to guess that they might well have been your best feature. Your lips that is. Your smile, well nothing could ever compare to that.

I do wish that I could see you again. Just the once.

Photographs and film are not the same.

They aren't you.

You can't smell a person from their photograph and you can't talk to them from their home videos. You can't touch them no matter what medium you use either.

If I could. If I could have you with me just one more time. I already know what I would ask.

I would ask you how your day had been. If you had encountered any unexpected difficulty at work and if you had managed to get time for lunch. I would ask you if you had spent the whole time that we had been parted thinking of me, of us. And I would ask you what you would want for dinner.

Just as I did every day.

Then you would ask me about my day in return. Interested in everything that I had done and every new development that had occurred in the company.

I would love that I suppose.

To experience it again. An ordinary day. With you.

To be completely honest, not to say that I would ever lie that is, but this topic is one of those few that I haven't been able to shake from my mind for some time now Rose. The dilemma of how you're truly getting on now. Wherever it is that you are out there in the universe.

If I is true that energy cannot be created or destroyed, I can remember that from science at least, and it is also true that the human soul – the essence of a person – is just electricity, then somewhere, somehow, you are still out there.

Or at least I hope you are.

And if that much is actually true. If one day I get to find out for myself. Then I have to ask you. How are you doing?

But asking you such a thing now, as I am at least, would serve no purpose now wouldn't it?

I honestly don't ever expect to get a reply. I don't ever expect for someone, even you, to actually read the words that I write in these letters. But I will keep writing them regardless of that truth.

For as long as I continue to, it's almost as though you're still here isn't it?

It's almost as though you're out there. Out there in the world. Somewhere. Just sitting patiently as you used to with the constant wait to hear from me yet again.

I like that idea.

I only wish that it was true.

Going into these writing sessions with the knowledge that no one will ever actually read them might have made some other writers give up by now. It might have made them realise that all they have been doing by continuing on in their effort to contact their departed loved ones was waste their time.

But I don't see it that way Rose.

Writing these letters to you, could never be a waste.

Even if they go unread for all of eternity, if they just sit in the chest on my bookshelf as they have done until they turn to dust, then I'll still be happy just by knowing that they existed.

That I didn't give up on you.

Even after you had gone.

I thought back on how we first met recently. Just the other day in fact. And looking back on it now, reliving it in my imagination exactly as it had happened in perfect clarity as I drifted off to sleep; filled me with such strong feelings of love and joy.

Just seeing you again like that, even if it was just in my mind.

It meant everything to me.

Just like you.

If I recall, we were both young adults at the time. Not even out of our teenage years yet either. It was spring, a warmer one than most back then and even perhaps by today's standards, but I do distinctly remember that it was peaceful that day. I could never forget.

The world around us both was so silent and calm that day. Almost no one out in town and almost no cars on the roads. And not even the slightest hint of sound from any of the windblown trees.

It was a Sunday now that I think about it more. It would have had to have been actually. You wouldn't have been anywhere near that old church if it wasn't.

I was just going about my business that day wasn't I?

I had no prior knowledge of what was about to happen and I defiantly didn't set out from home that morning to go and meet my future wife. I hadn't even the faintest idea of what was about to happen to me. It was all accidental. Or perhaps fate.

I was on my way to a job interview down the road whilst your Sunday group gradually flooded onto the street on their way home.

It was only by merest chance that we both became captivated by one another in that moment wasn't it? We have only a strong gust of wind and your hat flying off your head to thank for our meeting don't we?

The large beige summer hat, the one that flew from your head revealing your lush and beautiful brunette hair and the one that landed in my hands not more than three metres away.

You were so grateful for rescuing that hat for you that you demanded to know my name. I always thought that was odd. But judging by the age of that hat and the way that you held it, I would guess that it belonged to your mother. Didn't it?

So when I introduced myself and you replied with your name and a great amount of gratitude as you smiled and shook my hand, my first reaction was shock.

Today it would be rare to find even a handful of people per State with the name Rose. Back then it might well have been more. But it still wasn't a lot.

Your name was so unpopular and uncommon, that I knew it had to be you.

The first name of Rose, living in the same town where I had found the locket and the same eyes as the baby in the picture. I just knew that it had to be you. That after four years of waiting, in that moment I had finally found the owner.

But I never got the chance to ask you.

I looked down for what had to have been less than a second and when I looked back up, having pulled the locket from out of my pocket where I kept it almost as a good luck charm, you were gone.

I didn't even know how I had allowed that to happen,

But after that first meeting, I knew your face. I knew your smile. And I knew your voice.

And I also knew, that it wouldn't be long before I found you again.

But you know as well as I do, that it took a lot longer than I could have believed it ever would.

But I did find you again didn't I?

My dearest Rose.

LETTER

5

Dearest Rose

Recently, both the world and myself said goodbye to this past year. Welcoming yet another new one as we humans always do. Which makes it two thousand and six now.

It's not been over a year since you died. And that time has not passed quickly. It was slow, it was dull and it was depressing. Lonely. But I got through it. Which means that I can do it again.

I guess it means that I have to.

There were many celebrations, plenty of fireworks, a lot of singing and more than enough parties for anyone in the country to have had a good time.

But I didn't feel like celebrating. Not this year. Because I had nothing to look back on with a smile this time. Nothing that I could be grateful was finally over, because it's never going to be. Is it?

For me, that entire year had been spent picking up the pieces that you had left behind for me. It hadn't been fun, it hadn't been challenging. It had just been... hard.

So instead I sat in my office as I usually do these days, I held Jo on my lap and we watched the distant fireworks from the town over the hill from the safety and confinement of our now harrowingly chilled manor.

The night time winter's air is one thing to cope with at a time like this. But the lack of loving warmth from you being next to me in life and in bed is another entirely.

Even with the laughter that Jo causes and shares each day, even with her toys and her friends, the cleaners and the occasional hired chef, these halls are still too empty and quiet to sanely live inside without you here to fill them.

I realised it recently in fact but now you're gone from this world, the very sun above us all has at last lost its shine in my eye. It almost looks, empty.

It's funny. Or odd depending on how you define the word. But I know now that without that one thing in your life to devote all of your love, care and attention to day in and day out, the world around you becomes ugly.

Sick.

Infested with filth.

Human beings are a disgusting species when you look at them closely enough. Prone to war, poverty, famine, disease, pollution, discrimination, religion. The list could quite honestly fill the rest of this letter if I tried hard enough.

We are a snivelling child of a species. Doomed to kill our planet and scurry into the stars in search of another one to destroy all over again.

I can see that now.

Without you and your beauty, your clarity and your purity to shield and blind me from this madness that I have been foolishly convinced was acceptable as a way of life, I see now that I have always hated being human.

I do not hate my body, not my looks or my form. I do not hate myself, not my mind or my thoughts. But I detest and dislike how imperfect a machine our kind is.

We consume and we excrete waste over and over again

without end. Always taking, hardly ever giving back in exchange. Inventing newer and newer ways to kill our planet and each other with each passing year.

Humanity is a violent and untrustworthy species. Always looking out for itself and interested only in what a singular person can gain. Always lying, always fighting and always surviving.

Constantly developing new drugs and cures to illnesses that would have at one point kept our population in check. Habilitating the deformed and disabled, allowing them survive where they would have otherwise been thrown aside and allowed to perish in the hopes of making way for a fitting replacement...

I should probably stop now shouldn't I?

This way of thinking, this belief that humans and by extension myself and everyone I know are an unfit species isn't going to get me anywhere now is it?

I accept that humanity is not a species that any god could be proud of making but I also accept that I have much in my life to thank if for.

For all the pain, all the torment and anguish that I have been put through by being born amongst our species, there is such joy as well. So much happiness that far outweighs it.

I am thankful to have been born, because it allowed me to meet you.

I am grateful to have met you, because it allowed me to love.

And I am overjoyed to have loved you, because it gave me Jo.

Our darling little girl, our angel.

And she's just perfect.

My one remaining reason for being now that you are gone.

The source of all my smiles and laughter now. The focus of

most of my thoughts and the sole person in my life that I think I will ever love as much as I still love you.

She's going to be two soon. It's just a handful of months away now.

She's gotten so big. Oh Rose you I wish that you could be here to see her. To hold her and all her weight in your arms. I wish that you could talk to her.

Yes.

She can talk.

She started saying words just after nine months. Partially strung together sentences by sixteen. And now, at nineteen months she is so perfectly able to communicate that I think she might well go onto greatness later in her life.

I'm thinking of teaching her to read properly soon.

No more sounds and shapes on flash cards, but books.

I already read to her at night when she can't sleep. Just like you used to do before you passed. She loves her books, she gets so excited to see me reach for one off of her top shelf that her eyes almost come flying out of her head in amazement.

It's the cutest and most precious thing, her smile.

I wouldn't trade anything else in the world for it. Not even perhaps, seeing you once more.

I guess that as a father, that's just something that I'm never going to be able to give up. My daughter. And everything about her that makes her so special to me.

I wouldn't change anything, not one part of her, ever.

She's just perfect.

Healthy, walking, running, bumping into literally every piece of furniture when she's had even the slightest hint of sugar and always ready to play games with me and hide my things.

I can't tell you how many of my pencils and pens have gone missing but I do know that it's been enough that I actually had to buy more the other day. The first time that I'd done that in years.

She's mischievous, smart and funny. What more could I have asked for?

I take her out of the house and into the fields whenever I get the chance. Even if the weather is terrible. Which it often is. And she enjoys every moment of it.

Smiling, skipping and running around in puddles with her little green wellington boots and sparkly pink rain coat and giggling the entire time.

I don't think I've ever seen so much happiness in one person before.

It almost makes me feel ashamed that I can only observe her excitement, not actually feel it.

She'll be starting kindergarten soon. Getting proper social time with other children her age in a schooling environment. That's just over another year away and then she'll be ready.

Once I get her properly toilet trained of course.

She's been, a challenge to say the least,

Every time I think that I've done it right, she proves me wrong within a day.

I've spent weeks trying. Going through every trick in the books and following the advice of the doctors and nurses during her three month check-up recently but I've still had very little luck.

The furthest I've gotten so far is that she'll tug on my trousers and tell me when she needs to go but by the time she gets to the toilet with her little training seat, she's already been. And I have another diaper to change.

She'll get the hang of it soon though. I know she will.

She reached every other milestone on time or ahead of schedule so far, so this shouldn't be too difficult for her. She'll get there.

Actually she's reached a few milestones a bit sooner than I would have liked. Such as, quite unfortunately, the painting on the walls part of childhood.

We were playing with finger-painting the other week, just to see what she would think of having something like thick wet and cold paint all over her hands and as I looked away for three seconds to grab the phone, I hear an intense amount of giggling behind me. So I turn and what do I see?

I see a footprint in the paint, another one on the carpet leading the wall and her palm print. Her entire hand in fact. Pressed up against the wall. Marking it severely.

Though I can't blame her. She's only a child.

I wiped it off as best I could and had one of the cleaners, Sera I believe her name was, apply some more specialised chemicals to the blue tinge of that section later that night.

She didn't do any lasting damage but I doubt that you would have been too worried about that. You would be more concerned with the paint all over her hand wouldn't you?

Well fret not. I took her to the basin in the kitchen and washed her off properly. She didn't have a spec of the blue or purple paint left on her when I was done but she was plenty wet by the end of that trip and so was I.

She seems to enjoy splashing me with water and with how simple work has been recently I've had more than enough time to indulge her in any and every little game she's wanted to play.

I think the other admins at the company have finally accepted that my focus in life is my daughter now. Not the work. I've received less and less paperwork and phone calls over the months that it's almost obvious that they're finally taking on their part of the job.

But I guess that I did used to do as much as I could to lighten their load, so it's understandable that they would have needed time to adjust back to their actual routine.

But if I recall, we had a rule about talking to each other after a long day of work. That we would skip the subject entirely if it was going to be a long or complex discussion and just relax throughout our evenings together with that topic on the backburner for later in the night or perhaps the next morning.

I would think that this still applies.

However, I do miss hearing about your day.

Not that I would ever be so bold as to ask you directly since you never did like me prying but from time to time you would complain about customers at the shop or even your bitch of a manager and I would just sit there completely invested in every word you had to say.

I honestly loved every minute of it.

It was the highlight of almost every day.

I miss the little bits like that.

I miss you.

Jo though, as I had suspected, she unfortunately doesn't have any memories of you.

And now that she's coming along with her awareness of the world and her speech, I suspect that she will begin asking me questions soon. If the other children at her play groups and parks have mothers and fathers, or dual mothers or dual fathers – the world is changing more and more each day – then she's going to wonder why I'm all on my own.

However, there is another possibility.

Whenever I have to make an important call or deal with a visitor, Clorissa is always the one to watch over her should we have been in the middle of some game or bonding time.

She doesn't watch her for more than perhaps ten hours a

month at most and being a nanny isn't even an actual part of her job working as my assistant but she is always around at the right time and is always willing.

Says she loves the challenge. Apparently Jo reminds her of her younger sister when she was a baby. But considering that she's forty seven and her sister would be about your age now if she were still alive, that memory must be a rather old one for her.

I pay her extra and make sure to adjust her hours more considerately whenever she has to watch over Jo but she always protests. At the hour changes anyway, insisting that she have an increase rather than a reduction.

She must need the money. Surprising considering what she gets paid.

These days she spends a lot of her time in the central office though. Most of my communication with her has been through email and phone calls in the past few months but she does still check in on me from time to time and spend the day helping out as she used to when working from the manor.

Even she's worried I guess.

I am concerned though, that if Jo spends enough time around her in a parental fashion, then there is always the chance that she will become confused and start thinking that she's her mother.

I do hope that this doesn't happen though.

So as soon as I believe she's ready or she starts asking questions, I'll get out the scrap book.

The one that I put every picture we had that wasn't on display in for safekeeping a few years back.

I'll should start there.

Past that… well I have no idea yet.

I am making this up as I go. And with the move to China that the company is doing at the moment, my attention has been a little split. I haven't had a lot of mental capacity left to think ahead, I'm too focused on the present.

But I want you to know that we are both doing well my love.

I really want to reassure you of that.

And whatever this new year brings the two of us, I will face it with a level head and a smile and Jo will be protected from it all as she stands behind me.

You have my word on that.

My dearest Rose.

6

Dearest Rose

The strangest thing happened today my love. It's your birthday. But that wasn't what I meant. Obviously it felt strange not being able to celebrate a day that used to bring us both such joy and excitement from the cutting of your favourite Belgian chocolate cake to the singing of the song and the meals out with family and friends each year. There used to always be no end of entertainment surrounding this date in the past. I do miss that now.

And without you here. Without a reason to actually celebrate it anymore, instead this date now only brings me an excuse to simply pour myself a large glass of ice cooled bourbon and drink for the two of us as a toast to your memory now that that's all you are to me.

I suppose you might sum this up to say that I have found today's date far more similar to a repeating and very painful reminder of what I had lost in you rather than anything worth my own or anyone else's celebration.

Of course I invited your father again. I did that last year too, I'm not sure I remembered to let you know. But he and your mother refused. Best not to bring them back to the home where their child was always so full of life and happiness if the only thing waiting for them are the two people who killed her.

Also, I should say this at least, your father doesn't blame me or you for what happened my love. I asked him directly one night when I went round to see him. He doesn't even blame Jo, and the two of them get on very well whenever they do actually visit. But he does blame himself.

He's always felt guilty for being the one to take his own wife away from him and as your father, the one responsible for making you the way that you were, he's responsible in some way I guess.

Unlike my own sense of guilt, his isn't as unfounded I suppose.

Jo does enjoy his visits. I only with that both he and your mother could visit more. But with her business booming as of last year and his responsibilities within his own business becoming more and more serious as they expand further into the country, they like myself have simple been too busy to do so.

I'll make a better effort later in the year to get them in the same room with Jo more often. Even if Jo can't come, I'll make an effort to see your father anyway. He was always a good friend to me before you died.

I realise that the two of us have been distant in recent years but he'll come around. I can fix our friendship at the very least. I'd hate to lose my one good drinking buddy over something that neither of us were to blame for.

He was after all the only father that I have ever known.

Even if it wasn't by blood and even if he wasn't the one to actually raise me, I would have liked it if he was my father. I would have been proud to call myself his son. As I imagine you were to call yourself his daughter.

You did keep his name after all. You couldn't bring yourself to take mine could you?

Oh god, I wish that I could be discussing all of this to you in person rather than in a one sided conversation by letter. It's so hard to bring myself to say the words I want to say.

What I'm getting at, is that I care about the relationship between myself and your parents. Not just their relationship with Jo.

If possible, I would like to involve them both in the raising of our child as much as possible. She is their grandkid after all. They should get a chance to see her grow.

I never knew my parents, my grandparents neither. So for Jo to get the chance that I never did. To grow up with a father that loves her and two grandparents that love her just as much, would mean the world to me.

It would have only been made better if you could have been here too. It's a shame that you can't be. She'll surely miss you as she gets older. Especially when she gets to her teenage years.

I am certainly not looking forward to those.

Anyway. Back to the point of the letter eh?

It's your birthday, I already said but it helps me to get back into the flow if I mention it again. And whilst this date a year ago now, only a handful of months after your initial passing was indeed a challenge to get through at the time, this year it was overall a little easier to bear.

At least there was less crying involved on my part at both the stroke of midnight and when I remembered later in the day when I was alone. So that's an improvement if not the meaningfully significant change that I would have liked to make by now.

I would like it if I were able to look on days like this and whilst missing you more than ever, be happy for you. To be happy for the time that I got to spend with you, instead of just being sad that I can't have anymore.

I do miss you being here my love. I really do.

I wonder if there will ever be a day when I won't.

Actually… I live in dread of the day when I won't. Because that will be the day that I finally lose my compassion. My heart. My humanity and all the sanity of my mind.

Because no level headed or sane version of me could ever stop loving you. Even if you are now just a memory. Even if you had hated me in life, even if we had separated for reasons that I cannot even imagine, I would have still continued loving you.

So much so that I dare to say I'd have never met anyone else because of it. You were just too important to me to let go or replace. Even now.

It's been so different here without you that you wouldn't believe it. Almost like the world turns slower now, that the world is dimmer, quieter.

I'd dare say that life has lost its shimmer without you.

But that's just my perspective.

I wonder if your parents see if differently.

But I'd never be able to ask them something like that. Just imagine how that sentence would go. I'd anger your father and upset your mother in an instant. I can't do that to people I respect and care for. I'm just too kind a person.

I suppose that I should inform you, at least before I continue with the most important part of my message to you today, especially since she's already been mentioned. It would be cruel of me to keep you in the dark. But your mother, or at least your step mother to be specific and clear, has grown rather ill of late.

I realise that she could never replace your birth mother, in fact I would have been gravely offended if she had given the fact that I myself had never known my real parents and for someone to have willingly replaced them with new ones would have been the height of sin in my own opinion. But you did love her as though she were a true mother to you. I could tell just by how the two of you spoke.

Always telling jokes that were both secretive and for whatever reason entirely hilarious on both sides despite the fact that myself and your father never quite understood them. They were more than just inside jokes weren't they?

Something more special to the two of you?

Well whatever they were, it was obvious by watching the two of you laugh with one another every time that you were in the same room that you truly got along.

I can't recall the two of you ever arguing or fighting. Yeah you disagreed but it never got heated and you always managed to convince her to see your side.

And once you met me and stopped living off your mother's successful fashion carrier, the slight tension that existed between the two of you when it came to finances almost completely vanished.

Save perhaps from the wedding, you never once asked either of your parents for a penny. I was too quick to offer to spend my money on you for the thought to even occur.

From thanksgiving to Christmas, Easter and almost every other Sunday in-between, the two of you saw one another as often as you could manage didn't you?

She would come to us if your father wasn't available and you would go to her if I wasn't around. I almost found it touching really. How close you were to your parents.

Not overly attached or dependent on them but not rude, spiteful or *de*tached either. You were just in the middle. Exactly where I would have liked to be myself had I never grown up as I had.

But this lengthy letter is not about me. Actually I will rue the day that any of my future letters ever are. These letters are about you. They always will be.

Your daughter and the important parts about your life that I believe you would have liked to keep tabs on should you have been here. That's the point.

Now as I was saying.

Your mother isn't well I'm afraid.

I haven't had the chance to sit down with your father or any of the doctors and ask them exactly what's going on. All I have been able to offer him is my support as a friend whenever I get the chance. But with Jo, the company and the daily chore of keeping up my social connections, I haven't had as much time to be there for him as I would have liked.

All I know if that three weeks ago she entered the hospital bed that she sits in now and hasn't been able to leave it since dude to her condition.

She's conscious and fully alert but has been severely weakened by whatever it is that's effecting her.

The doctors are running every test that they can to get to the bottom of it and your father hasn't left her side for a second. Holding her hand the entire time. Almost obsessively.

Perhaps his experience losing one of his wives already has created a small excess of anxiety in him when it comes to his current spouse's health. I don't know for sure. I haven't gone through what he has.

Not yet and not ever.

I will never replace you.

You were far too unique for that.

I will try to get some time away from the company to take care of your father in the coming months if I can. For now however, China is beginning to be more of a problem than any of my partners or advisors had predicted and it's getting to the point where I might have to start doing more than just the occasional conference call when it comes to dealing with this.

I don't want to have to leave the country. Not if I would be leaving Jo and your mother behind. But if it comes to it, I may be forced to.

For the CEO to just refuse to meet with members of companies as powerful as his own on the grounds of personal commitments whilst still in his own country would more than likely lead to the total collapse of the deal.

I know that I shouldn't put my work first, I never have before, but this time I don't feel like I have been left with a choice. I apologise for that.

So that's your family updated at least.

Your father is eating well and healthy and your mother isn't dying just yet. However I do fear that it won't be long before that happens too. She's gotten so weak and thin in such a small span of time that it's infeasible to imagine any treatment working in time to save her.

I'm sorry to put it so blunt. But you never did like me lying to you for the sake of your feelings did you?

You always wanted the truth. No matter how cold and heart-breaking it was.

Actually I think that that's one of the reasons that we worked so well together. The fact that we never lied or had reason to. About anything.

Cooking, tastes in music and film, clothing. We never lied about anything did we?

Even if you would be cross with me for a while if I had told you my honest opinion about how much your tight dress wear would reveal your bosom and hips at the higher class parties, you still thanked me for sharing my view on it after the fact.

However that was always when you had had a few too many glasses of champagne so I'm not sure as to how truthful those words were. You were a bit of a loose cannon when intoxicated. Controllable for the most part and not at all embarrassing but I did have to be mindful of what you were saying when you were around me or talking about me to others.

Your sense of privacy and secrecy practically disappeared when you were drunk. The stuff that came out of your mouth even surprised you at times when I told you the stories.

But I did appreciate your honesty too.

About a lot of things.

All your past boyfriends and the more obsessive ones that I would have to look out for in the early years and all of your encounters with overly physical men when you went out with your friends to clubs.

I always loved the fact that I didn't have to question anything.

That I didn't have to worry.

It was almost like you were pre-emptively apologising at times. But you never had to. I don't recall a single time that you ever once did something that I was angry or disapproved of.

So you never had any cause for concern either.

But back to the point, and I promise that all of this connects to itself.

Today I had an interesting encounter with one of your old friends from college.

A Tim, Tim Roberts if I recall.

He went to the office looking for me, I wasn't entirely sure as to why he would try to reach out to me after so many years since that one time we fell out in a bar, and after my assistant sent him away, she informed me of his attempted forced entry of my personal office to try and find me.

I have no idea why he would have been so angry or so rushed to come and see me but there you go. That's what happened to me today.

Anyway, the interesting part about all of this, was that early this evening, several hours after he had visited the office, he arrived at my gate. Screaming into the call box to try and get in.

I have no idea how he found my address mind you.

I of course told him that I wouldn't let him anywhere near me until he calmed down and told me what this was all about and his response to this was to try and hop the fence in rage.

Which landed him restrained by our day security and arrested for trespassing within the time it took him to drop back down on the other side.

I'm not sure why he was here but once the police are done with him I'll give my contact in the local precinct a call to see if he knows anything more.

I do hope that you weren't keeping secrets form me back then.

Of course we had only just met properly at the time and weren't even dating but if this has something to do with you and your past then perhaps you weren't as honest as I thought you were with me.

Then again, this could all be nothing.

I don't mean to sound as though I am accusing you of anything but as far as it stands I hadn't seen or spoken to him in over twelve years before today. So I haven't a clue as to why he would come and find me now.

But regardless of all of that.

Happy birthday love.

I toast to you with bourbon once again as I write this.

It's 9:04 PM right now. Just a few minutes before your actual time of birth.

Jo is resting peacefully in her sparkly power puff girl's bed. Almost entirely bright pink with sequins and small plastic jewels all over it with pictures of her favourite TV show on the sides. It did cost a fortune so I expect her to like it.

I bought that for her birthday not too long ago now.

She found it early though so I had to give it to her then and there.

Three year olds are apparently smarter than I thought.

That was five or six months ago maybe.

Either way, she's doing well too.

Starting to get better on her feet, less reliant on my hand or the pram to hold her up when we go into the gardens for a bit of time in the mud or into town to meet some other parents so that she can go on play dates so she's improving all the time.

She's gotten so big too. I know I say this every time but you truly wouldn't believe it.

Her hand that barely managed to grip at my pinkie finger when she was born can now grab two of my fingers when their next to each other. And with a good bit of strength as well.

She's just starting to read a bit as well.

For a girl of only thirty eight months, the doctors say that's impressive.

She's going to be off to kindergarten within the next year and a bit. It's next September when she starts actually. Not too long now is it?

I can't believe it's gotten this far already.

It feels like yesterday that we welcomed her into the world and now she's already beginning to shape it to her will.

Deciding what her favourite colours are, her favourite music, food and clothes. Demanding bacon all the time when I'm in the kitchen.

Oh she's got a brilliant personality. So much so that I wish you could meet her.

I wish that she could meet you.

I've even started telling her stories of you now Rose.

The happy stuff, the simpler stuff at the very least.

I tell them as bedtime stories for now but when she gets a bit more intuitive and starts to actually ask in-depth questions about you, I will go further than that of course.

I want her to know you like I did.

And I won't leave anything out.

For now though.

Happy birthday again my love.

Here's to you.

My dearest Rose.

7

Dearest Rose

Have you missed me at all? Even a little?

And if you have, was it ever serious? Was it ever comparable, to how much I still miss you even now?

I'm sure that your life would have been as equally turned on its head had it been me who died and not you. But I can't imagine you holding on to me as long as I have you.

You were always so resilient. So adaptable.

If I had died and left you behind with Jo, I'm sure that eventually, even if it wasn't what you intended right away, you would find someone else. A woman as rare and unmatched in beauty as yourself would have had plenty of suiters to choose from with myself out of their way.

I believe that you've experience this before as it happens. Back in college when we were first dating. Even though you would tell the boys of the town that you were taken, they'd still try their hardest to woo you. They'd even tell you that they would be better than anyone else if you only gave them the chance to prove it.

And whilst I can't deny that there were more than a few boys then that might have been better looking or had nicer cars, the only real points of interest that a girl that age would have taken note of, you stayed with me. You didn't even give it a second thought.

I wonder if you had never met me, who you would have ended up with instead. I dare say that I have probably already met them. Even now, with the manor and the company, our ability to live wherever you want, we're still less than an hour's drive from the town where we both grew up. And it's a small town.

If you had ended up with any other man from there, I probably knew them at one point. I might have even called them friend at one stage.

Those first few weeks were fun though weren't they?

Keeping our relationship in the dark from all of your friends and my own. The staff and your parents for as long as possible. The secrecy from back then, the lies and the plans we came up with to sneak away whenever we could to spend the day, evening or night together, they were so invigorating that I began to get addicted to you even more because of them.

They were my drug back then. They were my high.

And you. You were my hook.

You drew me in with your good looks and intriguing personality and never let me go. You kept me on that line for as long as you could until I pulled myself out of the water once I had grown too impatient to keep waiting for you to get serious.

Let me explain.

We met because of your locket. That much we are clear on.

But the choice to actually start dating me, to become my lover before my actual girlfriend, that came after it. After I had finally worked up the courage to go against the status quo and ask you straight to your face and in front of all your friends to meet me privately to discuss something with you.

You know it makes me wonder. If I had been faster to tell you about it. To tell you that I had had your locket for almost six years by then, would I have still ended up where I did?

Would I have still had the time to become what I did to you?

Would I have even been interested?

It was only after watching you for a good year throughout the campus, deciding if it was really you and when it would be best to tell you what I had in my possession, that I gained my attraction to you.

After meeting you in front of the church too many years before for me to have been sure you would remember me, I was already aware of your physical beauty. But seeing you as a young adult. Watching you interact with other, seeing you laugh and enjoy your life. I realised that I needed to know more.

So I started stalking you.

Sorry but that's the best way to put it.

I followed you around school and town as much as I could to learn more about you and everything that I found out only made my interest grow. I dare say that when I did finally work up the courage to talk to you in person, it was the most terrifying thing that I had ever done.

There was me, someone who had been doing his best to meet you for a good six years of his life, and you, someone who barely knew me, who didn't even bat an eye when you caught me watching you.

I'm surprised that you said yes to me as I was then.

I was obsessed with you and you knew it.

What was it that possessed you to trust me?

It couldn't have been attraction or intrigue. It couldn't have been out of pity or to humour me. And it couldn't have been to set me up because you did show. So what was it?

Had I missed something?

Were you… watching me when I was watching you?

Or was it something else?

I wish that I could ask you in person. I even tried a few times. But the conversation never flowed naturally enough for me to bring it up with you. And every time I went to say the words something else come out entirely.

I feel ashamed for that.

That even after I had gotten to the point of marrying you, I was still too much of a coward to question you directly about something as simple as this.

I could have just asked "why me".

I could have just come up to you at any point after I had met you and asked you what had consumed you to take me at my word and meet me alone like you did.

If I could go back and change things, I would change that.

And other than your death, that's probably the only thing that I would ever want to change. Because everything else was perfect. I only wish that I could have known you longer. That I had met you at a younger stage.

Anyway, this touching display of my true feelings on paper is not the actual reason for my writing you today. Actually I sat down to write this so that I might ask you a different question.

Because I've been wondering as of late. As I often do about many things. But I wasn't to know. Can you hear me, even now? Praying to you each night before I set down to sleep through yet another cold turn of the darkness before daybreak just a short few hours later?

Can you hear me calling out your name?

Screaming internally for you to return?

Or are my words just fading away as I say them now? Never to be heard by anyone but myself and anyone else listening in. I wonder if this is the case. Because no matter how I try to contact you now my love, you're not there to answer me anymore. I know that's how it is now but I'm fearful that this is how it will always be.

I don't want that to be the case.

I *do* know that you're gone, I know that you're dead. I could never forget. But I'm still struggling to accept it in my heart if not my mind.

Even now, over three years since it happened, I can still hear your voice in the background noise of the house Rose. I can hear you calling to me.

I can still feel your warmth beside me in bed when I first wake up in the mornings. I can still smell your perfume and your scent on the sheets and the couch.

I can even still taste your lips. And picture your perfect hips.
Sorry for the rhyme.

If I can still hear you. If I still feel as though you *are* still here, just somewhere and somehow out of my arm's reach, hiding within these endless halls just out of view, waiting for me. Then is it the same for you?

Can you hear me? Can you feel me?

My love, my compassion, my desire and my conviction?

My loyalty?

Can you feel any of that now Rose?

Can you feel anything at all in the first place?

I don't even know what it's like for you now.

What can you see? What can you hear? Taste, smell, feel?

I truly wish that I could know.

To be able to see that you are out there, somewhere, looking down on this world or even on myself, perhaps on some alien shore that I myself will never get to see, would fill me with such relief.

To know that you're not suffering whilst I live down here in the torment of my loss instead of you. To know that you're safe. To know that in some way, small or largely philosophical, you were still living. That you still had a life. Even if you weren't strictly speaking alive.

I've been reading various religious texts recently.

All of them.

My psychiatrist that the shareholders forced me to employ over concerns for my mental wellbeing tells me that it's my attempt at searching for some form of answers to questions that were not meant to be asked. But I think differently about it all.

I'm not looking for answers, I know that you're out there somewhere, I can feel it. But what I am looking for is a window. A keyhole. To experience what life is like for you now from my own end.

I thought that if I were to go through every piece of imagery and description of the afterlife both the good and the bad then I might be able to piece them all together and manage to picture some compilation of them all as to roughly imagine what you see now.

But it hasn't worked.

Yet.

I intend to keep trying though.

I feel that I owe myself and your memory that much at the very least.

I've found myself thinking of you more than I would normally do recently even regardless of this secondary research project.

Not just because it's been another Christmas, new year and birthday without you as well. Not even because it's been another birthday for Jo as well, but because today, September ninth, two thousand and eight, she started school.

She was so excited, and I was so nervous.

All those mothers, single or in a partnership, waving goodbye to their little angels as though they never expected to see them again, it seemed wrong to think that you weren't there too. It felt wrong to be one of the only single fathers there as well.

It felt wrong to receive all those concerned and sympathetic looks when they saw my sad face looking at our own little angel walking away from my arms and into the room with her new teacher and fellow classmates.

You see for the first time in four years, I wasn't having to leave her whilst I was busy with work or some social affair, I was being left behind by her whilst she was busy with her own life.

And although it's only just begun, I can already imagine the woman that she will one day become later on in it. And I only wish that you could have been here to see that too.

Truthfully today was the most terrifying six and a half hours of my entire life.

The constant thought that Jo might get hurt or be bullied. What if she didn't fit in because she didn't have a mother? What if she got too much attention because of her family name? I was scared of everything.

I was so worried that she wouldn't be able to cope with parting from me for such a period of time that I kept my keys next to me and the gate unlocked on the off chance that I had to bust out of the door and go get her as soon as the school rang.

But they never did.

Instead I left at three, picked her up at three thirty and took her home.

She was as full of energy as she had been when I had

dropped her off but she was noticeably different. Changed.

Smiling more, curious of everything and somewhat more obedient too.

I am curious as to what the staff did in there to make her like this but she shows no signs of harm or neglect, she said that she had eaten the lunch that I packed for her and she said that she had had plenty to drink so whatever this change signifies, I believe it to be an omen of positivity rather than anything sinister as my pessimistic mind would have had me believe.

She is the perfect child though.

A mother even complimented me when she was waiting with all the other kids waiting to go in. Telling me that she was gentle and considerate of others. Especially when it came to their personal space.

I thought it odd for her to have noticed that within only a handful of minutes but if it was that obvious then I suppose that I've done a good job in raising her so far. And I will endeavour to continue succeeding as the years press on.

To think that Jo has come this far. Started school, reached the age of four. Tying her own laces for once. Although she claimed to have forgotten how to do it the very next day. It's amazing.

She never seems to be upset about anything anymore too. And as the months have gone on lately, she has been asking about you. And this time I mean actually asking.

Questioning what you would have done in certain situations and what you would have thought about her clothing choices. Just like any curious little girl would.

It'll be time to get the scrapbook out soon I guess.

She hasn't seen it yet so I can only guess as to how she will react but I'm intrigued more than I am concerned. I almost can't wait to give it a try.

However, whilst our little bundle of joy might be the most

important thing in both our lives from a certain standpoint. There is more that I must inform you of my love.

Starting with your mother.

Her illness has grown more severe in recent weeks.

She spent almost three months in hospital last year, having every test done and ending up without a definite diagnosis and just some pills to help her gain back her practically non-existent appetite.

This time however, they found the diagnosis in mere hours.

And I'm sorry to say that it's not good news.

She has cancer Rose. I'm so sorry.

It's stage three, beyond operable, spreading quickly and centred in the stomach.

It's unlikely that she will make it the rest of the year. And I can only think on this and realise that I am for the first time grateful that you died when you did. Because now you won't have to watch this as myself and your father are.

I visit him most days now. Work allowing of course.

We sit in the back yard, share a beer and perhaps even fire up the grill for a few hours each visit. He seems to enjoy the company now that your mother is bed ridden in hospital over an hour's drive from him. And he always enjoys seeing Jo.

He visits your mother at a minimum of three times a week but he can't stay there constantly. She won't allow it and the hospital defiantly won't either.

In her words, he's not allowed to drag his own life into the ground just because hers is finally ending. And for once, I have to agree with her.

I know that we didn't always see eye to eye in the early years of our relationship. Your mother and me I mean. I guess it's because she isn't as naïve as your father. She knew full well what we were up to near the end of our teen years.

But for once, I agree with what she said.

Like what you made me promise you near the end, I can't allow my life and by extension the life of our daughter suffer without you here. Telling me that it would be rude of me not to at least try to manage on my own.

She's now made your father give her a similar promise.

I do promise you now however. That no matter what happens, I will support your father.

As a friend. A bank. A punching bag or a cook. Whatever he needs from me he shall have it. He's family. And I don't turn my back on family.

It would be wrong of me to.

This is the only family that I've ever known. I could never ignore any of it in such a dire time of need.

However I should mention Rose. Your father isn't coping as well as I have. Remember I said we would share a beer? Well it's more like I would have one for every five that he went through each time. And I know that he's drinking more than that when I'm not there as well.

I emptied his bins one time. There was no end of vodka and gin in there. And this was from a single week. I have no idea how much he's going through in a month. But it defiantly isn't safe. Not for his health or his mind.

I'll try and get him to slow down if not see someone to help him as soon as I get the chance.

If he refuses, then I'll get him out of the habit myself.

A strong mountain of a man like him shouldn't be lowered to such levels. Even if it is the end of his world. I'm not letting Jo grow up without at least one of her grandparents and I am not allowing a man whom I look up to as my own father slowly take his own life right in front of me like this.

Ah… This really isn't the year that I was hoping it would be to be honest.

China finally fell through, your mother ended up back in hospital, I had to send our child off to school for the first time in my life and hers and recently another hardship made its way to me.

Your old friend from college. Tim.

Well he got in touch again a few weeks back.

After I dropped the charges for trespassing and had him released he just refused to speak to me. Probably out of some form of spite. So I left it at that. But then I received a call from him. Direct to my office phone.

I can't remember exactly what he said but I do remember his tone. And at least two of the words defiantly stuck in my mind once I had heard them.

"My child!"

If he thinks he can make any form of claim over my daughter without ground then my lawyers will dig him a ditch so deep that he'll be able to see Australia before I'm done.

But if it's at all possible that it's true...

If something happened between the two of you that I don't know about. Then I don't know what to think.

I'm not one to accuse. But this has made me worry.

What if you weren't as honest with me as I thought you were?

I really hope that this isn't the case.

Because if it is, I'll still love you.

I just don't know if I'll still be able to trust you.

My dearest Rose.

LETTER

8

Dearest Rose

I learnt something truly spectacular today my love. Something so wonderful that I cannot begin to imagine anything better in all the world.

Something that was so life changing to me, that at the same time it became equally sorrowful as well. Because today I heard our darling angel sing for the very first time in her life and my own. And it was so beautiful. A sound and an experience that I believe I will never come across again.

Because for the first time since you've been gone. For the first time since I met you in fact. I have seen actual beauty again. I have found myself something besides you and your personality that I now consider pretty.

I have found something precious.

And now that I have found it, I never want to let it go from my hands and arms. Not if I can help it.

I don't even know how she knew the words. Actually I didn't even think she had an interest in music until it happened. But I'm so glad that it did.

I was driving her to school this morning, it was the beginning of her second week there today as well and irregardless of that fact, it was a big step for her anyway. Because today was the first day that she had to tell me it was time to go.

I was three minutes behind our regular schedule and when she heard me say that I was running late because of work, she freaked. Forced me to put down the paperwork in my hand and practically marched me to the car.

She's so bossy that I almost mistook her for you.

But back to the point. We were in the car, on our regular route and due to arrive with plenty of time before the gates opened and when I reached over to turn the radio from whatever new pop song it was playing to the business station, she told me to stop.

She said that she liked it.

So I turned it up and in the background of this heavy beat and mesmeric vocal track, I heard the gentle hum of a familiar voice singing along. When I listened closer, not taking my eyes off the road for a moment, I quickly realised that it was her.

It was Jo's voice. Jo's singing.

And as I gradually tuned out the actual music to listen more closely, I was instantly taken aback by how perfect it sounded tp my ears. Mind you it was obviously off tune and a bit amateur as you would expect but it was well paced and perfectly synced to the music. It even had the same emotional flare as it as well.

It truly was an amazing thing to experience this morning.

How I wish that you could have been here to hear it too.

Besides this moment today though, life here on earth has been fairly in check recently. From my point of view anyway. However limited that may indeed be.

I should tell you that I was finally able to put a few hours in at work for once. The first time that I've been to the office for anything more than a signature or social event in the entire three years since you've been gone.

They were surprised as I was to be there. I hadn't even

planned it really. I just heard what was going on there – the state that everything had been allowed to fall into without my oversight on every department day by day and felt that I had to step in before it was all too late for me to rectify it all at a later date.

And I found that myself and the company had yet another surprise waiting for us bothy when I got there.

The Chinese ambassador. Along with his full diplomatic motorcade, was sitting outside of the building's entrance blocking a large portion of the road whilst he was waiting for me to arrive.

I wasn't even told to expect him. Actually I wasn't expecting him at all. It was entirely spontaneous of him to visit. My assistant was actually just in the middle of dialling my number when I signed into the system in the lobby.

Now I'll spare you all the heavier details and most of the specifics, I know that you never had any real interest in them and I know that a lot of them used to fly over your smiling and nodding head when I did talk about them.

But he was there to propose a deal with me.

You see a very powerful man in the Chinese government had managed to overrule the decision to refuse my company entry to their market and had sent the ambassador, a close friend apparently, to talk me through the new deal with the express instruction to inform me that should there have needed to be any amendments, I would still have their full support depending on how reasonable they were.

For a company like mine, one specialising mainly in electronics manufacturing to the US and some other allied countries, to have been allowed entry into a market like theirs was a once in a life time opportunity. It was for anyone I guess. But even though the contract was vague, I accepted it then and there since neither I nor my lawyers could find any issues with it that would need any immediate attention or more of the ambassador's time.

So with that done, signed, hands shaken over it and pictures of the event taken for legal purposes, the deal was at last complete. And we were finally in.

They, being the Chinese government or whomever it was in the country that had gotten their attention, were interested more in our agricultural connections and business models than anything else that my company had to offer them but they welcomed the proprietary and powerful technology that we could bring them by working alongside their top suppliers as well.

The whole reason that the company wanted this in the first place wasn't to expand or to turn more profit but to be able to lower our expenses and in turn lower our product costs to our customers. Eventually allowing us full domination of the market in which we inhabited.

If we can get our microchips and machines out the door cheaper than we can already then they'll sell much faster. Giving us more business and establishing our name across the glove much faster than ever expected.

With the abundance of cheap land to build manufacturing plants on in China as well as the readily available labourers and the almost tax free rare metal purchases, we should be able to lower prices by as much as ten percent. Without costing us a penny.

You always liked that about the company didn't you?

That we weren't out for a profit but instead interested only in higher sales?

For as long as I've owned the company, the electronics portion at least, we have only ever made a three percent profit per year. Just enough to offset inflation and business tax.

That was the point to it all I suppose.

Developing technology to not only make dangerous jobs safer but to also offset the physically demanding parts of manual jobs without entirely removing the human element for as cheap as we could and as affordable as we could was always the driving ambition in my mind when I started down this road. And now here we are. The number four commercial business in the US in terms of total value and soon to be number three if we can increase our gross income by another two percent this quarter. Making us work in total, almost six hundred billion dollars.

Impressive eh?

It's defiantly a lot of zeros.

Mike, the shareholder directly below me in terms of how much he controls the company, was very happy about that fact. But you would know him better than me. You two were the best of friends before you died. I dare say that you spent more time talking to him than you did me whenever the two of you were in the same room.

He may own twenty three percent of the company and I may only own sixty four, but I value his opinion greatly when it comes to the direction we move the business in. And in my own opinion, without his help and connections, we would have never been in a position to attempt a move to China in the first place.

I should thank him for that at some point.

We're celebrating the deal with China next month when it becomes official and public to the rest of the world. I'll see if I can get a few minutes on stage to give a speech then if I remember to. I bet he'll love being called out like that. He's never been one for the spotlight and I'm going to point quite a few at him as soon as I mention his name.

Anyway.

You remember how in my last letter I told you of what Tim Roberts told me in his phone call with me last week right? How he had claimed that Jo was in fact his own child and not mine?

Well there've been a few developments in that case. Specifically the fact that it's become a case. He's taking me to court over it. The possession of my own daughter.

Which is what ultimately forced me to finally bite the bullet.

I had my lawyers look over it all as many times as they could but there was no way to avoid a court date with this man unless I had proof to disprove his claims and have the case thrown out on the grounds that it was all false.

So I had to take the test.

I went into our local clinic, had them draw some of my blood and Jo's and have been waiting patiently for the results for three days now.

At least, I had been waiting patiently. Because a few hours ago, I got the call that I had been waiting for. I've got the results.

But first, I should explain a little.

His version of the story is that one night in a bar a year before you died, the two of you met up. You were both drunk and a hotel was involved. One in which neither of you used any birth control.

I have no way of knowing if this is true. It certainly doesn't sound like the woman that I knew to have just jumped back into bed with an old boyfriend when you had been happily married for over a decade. But that wasn't the point.

The point was that the times lined up.

He had the receipts to prove that he had spent the night there on that date and he also had the date of Jo's birth to prove that the timeline matched. Which for the judge he took this too, was more than enough to get it in court.

But now I have proof to the contrary. Because I have DNA evidence that I personally requested to be ran five times with different samples of blood in each case; that irrefutably proves without any doubt that Jo *is* my daughter.

So whatever happened that night with Tim. I don't care.

I hope you understand that I felt as though I had no choice but to do this. I had every confidence that Jo was my daughter before I went into this but I had to be sure. I legally had to be sure.

You see Tim had some shoddy legal letter sent to my doorstep instructing me that he would be taking me to court by tomorrow if I didn't offer up proof that she was mine.

So of course I did the test simply because he forced me to.

Even if he had managed to get me to prove that she wasn't mine. She was still my daughter. And I would have fought tooth and nail to keep custody of her. And with my legal team, there was no way that I would have lost that battle.

You know that first hand.

You came to court with me once over a patent dispute if you remember. And you saw then exactly what my lawyers are capable of when they've been given enough of my money to line their pockets.

But I didn't need them this time. I was sure that I was her biological father so I took the test without any fear that it wouldn't come back as I was expecting. But I did not expect what else I found out when this was all over today.

And it is for that reason alone, that I know you too would have wanted to hear what I am about to tell you.

Not only is she my daughter, in fact she's so close to my own DNA that she might as well be a sister rather than my child, but she's clear.

Of everything.

She's clear of everything.

Every hereditary disease known to man.

Every congenital illness that's possible for her to have.

She's completely healthy and strong.

And she's luckily not even a carrier of the disease that took you from me Rose.

She's safe to have kids.

And her kids are safe to have kids.

The doctors said that they didn't understand how it was even possible. But she has no trace of what is yet still an entirely unknown and frankly little understood disease.

But now that we know, you don't have to worry.

She's safe.

And I want you to know that I'll be presenting this evidence in court and in person tomorrow at the preliminary hearing with the judge and Tim.

I want to know his side of the story in full and look him in direct in the eye as he speaks before I go ahead and prove to him that none of it's true.

I just want to understand the full picture and whether or not all of this is a lie before I go ahead and force him out of my life and Jo's for good.

But even if it does come out that you actually did have an affair, or even a one night stand as he claims, I don't care anymore. No one's perfect, well perhaps you were closer than others, but everyone in life makes mistakes. Even me.

We're all human.

An imperfect creature by design.

So I don't even have anything to forgive you for.

You did nothing wrong.

I know that I was always busy with work in the early years

and even more so as time went on and I know that I wasn't really as affectionate as I could have been back when we first met in college, but I made up for that I think.

At least I hope I did.

I don't know. Maybe I'll get to ask you one day.

What kind of a husband I was to you.

I really hope that I get the chance to do that.

I really hope that, when I die, even if it's just for a split second or in my subconscious, that I get to see you again Rose.

I believe that I deserve that much at least.

Now. I've got Jo to see to and a lot of plans to approve for the business model in China that should get to go into effect late next year if all goes to plan. So for now Rose. I leave it at this.

I'm always thinking about you.

And I'll always love you.

You were and are everything to me.

And from now until for ever. You will always be-

My dearest Rose.

LETTER

9

Dearest Rose

You know Rose, something happened today. Something that I've been anticipating for a long time now. Because the time finally came for me to tell that story today. The story of how we first met. And before I could even start, it got me thinking. How did we really meet?

At what point in our intertwined lives and destines should we define as the one singular moment when we actually stood face to face and learnt each other's names and personalities?

At what point did we really meet not only the people that we were on the outside, but the ones that we cling to more deeply than ever when we're alone on the inside?

I wasn't really sure to be honest.

Which is why I ask you now.

Nineteen eighty four.

That was when our story started wasn't it?

The day that you lost your locket?

I didn't know it then but by finding this small piece of gold and brass amongst the dirt that day would at one point much further down the life in my life, change my whole world forever.

If I had to choose, I would say that this point was the most important of them all. The teenage me, finding the locket that had been dropped by the teenage version of you. But it wasn't where we met. Not by a longshot.

That was just how this all began.

Fast forward three years further then. And we find ourselves at nineteen eighty seven, specifically the day that the two of us casually crossed paths for the first official time in the street outside the St. Jude Baptist church in our home town.

It was a Sunday then. The most important Sunday that I will probably ever experience. The day that you're oversized and pricy summer hat flew off of your perfect little head at the age of sixteen and blew directly towards me as I stood several feet down the path from yourself just minding my own business at the time.

I caught it for you, then presented it back to you as you suddenly approached and for the first time, that was when we spoke to one another. Nothing but a short and sweet exchange of names and words of gratitude before your father and his then girlfriend summoned you back to their side before taking you back to what I assume would have been your home.

I would have introduced myself properly then had I the chance. I would have told you the truth about who I was. And I how we were connected. But I was too slow and scared then to even try.

I was just a simple seventeen and a half year old boy with almost no experience talking with women or in the department of love and defiantly no experience with those with a figure befitting that of an angel.

I would have done my damnedest to tell you who I was and why it was so important that you speak to me if I had actually managed to get any of the words out through my tense stance and plum red embarrassed face had I been given that chance. But it wasn't the time for such things back then. And I'm glad I never got the chance to screw it all up as well.

I doubt that it would have gone very well and I highly doubt that you would have actually listened to anything that I had to say. But if the chance had arisen for me to present you with that locket hidden deep within my back pocket where I kept it most of the time both as a lucky charm and for the chance to give it back to the owner one day should I have ever found him, even though I had no idea it actually belonged to you, I know that you would have stayed around to hear me out.

But you were gone almost as quickly as you appeared after that weren't you? Just like the wind. Beautiful, pristine, and impossible to grab a firm hold of.

But after that moment I knew your face, I knew your name and I knew your church. It was only a matter of time before I found you again as far as I could see it back then. But the chance never came around did it?

Not for two whole years. Making it nineteen eighty nine. When we had both just enrolled at the same college however not the same course within weeks of each other without any preplanning or thought given to the subject.

It had just happened that way by coincidence hadn't it?

I would see you from time to time in the halls. A dazzling eighteen year old woman walking amongst her friends and always being sought after by man after man, never opening herself up for someone like myself to ever make it near.

But I could never be sure.

I would have sounded odd back then.

For someone that you had never really met before, to have come up to you, remind you of that random time you had almost lost your hat in the street and then presented you with a locket he had found three years before even than in the hopes that the one Rose he knew of in all of town might have ended up being you.

I would have been the laughing stock of not only that school but every other one in the country after that if my hunch wasn't correct. It would have probably been known as the worst chat up line in all of history as well.

And a small part of me thanks how sheepish and shy I had been back then for not putting either of us through such embarrassment.

But you remember the true way that it happened in the end don't you? The moment that I would guess we actually met one another after all of those years?

It was six months into the semester, we were on break, and for whatever reason during that summer, I had gotten the idea to go down to the swimming pool for a change. And you, you were there.

Alone.

Stood with your towel and costume carrying bag in your hand waiting for your father to come and pick you up after an exhausting few hours in the water. But he was running late that day. Enjoying his date with your future step mother a bit too much to have remembered to come and get you on time.

So as I went to enter the long line of families and the regular visitors for the pool, I spotted you stood up against the back wall of the building. Still dripping wet.

I saw it as my only opportunity to talk to you properly so I took the chance that had been presented to me and I gripped it as tightly as my hands could manage.

"Excuse me... miss?" I asked you, not fully gaining your attention as you had no doubt assumed I was talking to someone else by how polite I was being to you. "Rose?"

You looked up to me, immediately staring at my face to try

and place me now that you believed I in some way knew you since I had spoken you name.

"You probably don't remember me but..."

"The guy who saved my hat one spring. Right?" You asked me in return.

"That's right yeah." I told you. "There's something that I've been meaning to ask you since that day actually. Something important."

"I don't have time to turn down anymore guys today. Sorry."

"It's not like that. Honestly." I pleaded.

"Then what?" You asked.

"Did you lose a locket, in eighty four?" I asked you with uncertainty.

"Might have done... why?" You asked with apprehension and curiosity.

"I know where it is. I normally have it on me but not today as it happens." I explained.

"Really?" You asked me almost sarcastically, probably not believing a word. "And I assume you want me to get in your car and go home with you to find it?"

"I don't have a car and I doubt that any girl your age is that stupid. Trusting a stranger is never a good idea." I reassured you.

"Then what do you want?"

"Just give me a phone number and I'll arrange to meet you somewhere public if you like. The café that just opened a few streets from here perhaps?"

I still can't believe that that worked but I did get your digits in the end didn't I?

I called you just hours later and set the time and date for our meeting. Assuring you that I would be coming alone and that I wasn't against you bringing anyone else with you as a way of feeling safe.

I really wasn't expecting you to also turn up alone though.

You really thought that I was misleading you didn't you?

Your first words to me then were more than enough to prove that.

"So, what are we really going to do today?" You asked with intrigue. Almost gleaming with excitement as you expected me to be taking you on some overly pushy and cheesy romantic trip around time

"What do you mean?" I inquired.

"Well this was all a ruse to get me on a date right? Others have tried a lot less before and it's worked. You though, I don't even know how you could know about the locket..."

So I handed you the locket and watched your mind blow apart in surprise.

It was the first moment that I ever saw you like that. And thankfully, as we sat and talked for hours that day about how I had found it and what I had been doing with it over the years, asking everything about you and your mother as I had been dying to know for the better half of a decade, we realised that whilst we had very little in common, we got on well together.

So well in fact, that I didn't even have to beg you for the second date. You called me two days later and demanded it. And ever since, our adventures on those days that we did spend together before your father found out and interrogated me for a full week before I would be allowed to see you again, were the best moments of my life.

I will tell you of them again soon my love.

As for now, duty calls.

We have a daughter to raise after all.

And as her sixth birthday is in just a few days' time. I have a lot of work to do.

However, I should tell you.

Your mother. Your step mother.

She passed away this morning. I suppose that's why I felt the need to write to you again out of everything.

After battling with her cancer for three years, she finally succumbed to it.

I want you to know that she wasn't in any pain, she wasn't alone in her final moments and she wasn't at all sad.

She welcomed her end.

And hopefully now, she's up there with you.

Laughing by your side once more.

At least I hope she is.

My dearest Rose.

10

Dearest Rose

Do you know what it feels like know? This emptiness inside? The one created when you passed from this world and left me behind. Alone.

Do you have any idea how it feels to not have you here with me anymore? How it feels to carry on as a widower seven years after you died?

There is no short way of describing it.

The emotions are just too powerful. Too potent.

Too complex.

You and I know full well that I've gone on about this more than enough over the years in these letters and lord knows I've tried to stop myself from bringing it up each time but I have found now that it's simply too difficult a challenge to overcome on my own anymore.

To ignore the feelings deep inside of me even now.

You were like the sun to me. Something that was so fundamentally essential to my continued existence that without you with me I fail to see any point in even struggling on just for survival at all. Because it wouldn't be what I once called living. Not without you here.

You filled every room with such warmth and gave me such comfort whenever I heard your voice that my days have truly not been anything similar to what they once where since you left me behind.

I think that it's reached the point where it's been too long now my love. Where I've spent too long without you to keep on just barely coping as I have been.

It's been far too long since I've seen your smile, since I've felt your soft cheeks that would blush at almost every opportunity and fan my hands along your slender figure.

It's been too long since I've seen your shining hair that would stand out even in the densest of crowds and it's been far too long since I last heard you laugh.

I've spent too long without you.

I can't even imagine how I've managed to make it this far.

To think that it's already been seven years. I can't believe that it's taken this long to realise this but at last I want it to stop here. I cannot go another moment without you with me. I refuse to.

But I know that I must.

Because I made you a promise and I owe it to Jo to keep it. I will be here for her as her father until she is at the very least good and ready to take care of herself without my continued support. That is the absolute height to what I have to reach before I can be allowed to die.

Until I can come and find you again.

But even then.

Who's to say that she'll actually let me go that easily?

It's not like I could just raise her with a set date of my death in place. I don't even know when the time will come for me to make that choice. But I do know that it's going to happen. I simply can't live like this anymore.

I've said it a thousand times and would gladly say it a thousand more if it would bring you back to me but it remains true even to this very day, that you were my everything. And by dying, that is what was taken from me.

I didn't just lose a wife, a friend and a sexual partner. I lost a soulmate.

A reason for living, a reason for getting up each day at the crack of dawn. My reward for a hard day's work and the one person in the world that I would ever feel safe sleeping next to each night.

You were my reason to smile. My excuse to laugh.

My reason to be happy.

You remember it right?

How shy I was when we first started dating; especially when we first spent the night together? How apprehensive and shaky I was just at the thought of getting under the sheets with you? A beautiful and fully naked nineteen year old girl?

It wasn't even the sex that scared me. That was the easy part really. It was what came after that I was afraid of. It was trusting the person sleeping jus on the other side of the bed, just behind my back, to not be some form of monster in disguise that would reveal themselves once I was unconscious.

I was scared of sharing the bed not my body.

Isn't that strange?

To not at all be the least bit embarrassed to take off my clothes in front of a girl or to commit no end of sexual acts each night but instead to be truly terrified of allowing myself to fall asleep next to her in the hours that followed. It's so irrational that it might as well be childish.

I was trembling that night though. You must have noticed.

Shaking in my skin with my mind fully alert for hours as you just casually fell asleep behind me.

Clinging to my covers with my eyes wide open, staring intently at the clock on my wall as I impatiently awaited for my own time to come, thinking that it I just sat there long enough I too would finally get some sleep.

But it never happened.

I stayed awake and in the same singular position that whole night.

I was so tried the next day that I have to fake an illness to try and get you to leave me to rest. I even had to call in sick at work just so that I could be left alone long enough to get a minimum of eight hours sleep in before I gave up on even that a relied on caffeine to keep me awake.

But that's not exactly what happened is it?

You were so worried about me that morning that you stayed with me the whole time. So concerned over my wellbeing that you stayed, in the bed, the whole time.

You offered me no end of hot drinks, soup and even a hot towel and you tried again and again to make me as comfortable as you could. But I told you at every attempt that all I needed was more sleep. And so you got back under the covers, and remained like that for hours more. Holding me.

In truth you being there should have made the whole situation worse for me but somehow, laying there half dead from exhaustion, listening to your soft voice and your shallow breathing, it actually helped.

You see Rose?

You see how important you were to me?

You were the person who finally got me over the fear of sleeping next to another human being. You were the one person in all my life, that I had ever felt comfortable sleeping alongside.

You were such an important part of my life that it's hard to fully describe it. Even on paper with all the time in the world to get my words out.

And now you're gone.

You've been gone for a while.

Seven years.

Seven years today.

I buried your cold, silent and lifeless body in the chilled earth below that old church seven years ago this morning. You died a little over two months before that. But it is this day that gets to me the most. Because it is this day that I had to actually had to say goodbye.

The anniversary of the day that I had to stand in front of a room full of our family and friends and speak my chosen words of solemn remorse as I summed up the value of your life and the complexity of my emotions towards you in what ended up being just a little less than ten minutes. To do all of that and then have to bury you. That was my goodbye.

And I look back on it now and think to myself often.

That I could have done better.

I could have said more or perhaps even less. And I think that I could have been at least a little bit gentler towards your father as well. I could have been kinder to your mother and to your friends also now that I think about it. And I could have done less to alienate them from my life.

But I couldn't help myself on that day.

I had just lost my wife and had a small daughter to look after alone from then on. How could I bring myself to appear kind to any of them on that day? I was grieving, and I wasn't coping with it well.

So I remained closed off and snapped at anyone who tried to get close and offer their shallow remorse. And I was like that for the entire day. I wish I hadn't been now. I actually liked a few of the people I pushed away.

Losing you hit me harder than it did most of the others I guess. So my acting out *stood* out even more because of it. Then again you were always a much bigger part of me than you were to them. But looking back on it now I shouldn't have reacted as I did. I shouldn't have said what I did.

Perhaps I'll have the courage to actually tell you that story one day.

But with the anniversary of this mistake coming and passing in the early hours of this morrow, I have found myself thinking back on it once again. Just as before.

I would like to be able to tell you that it's gotten at least a little easier as the years have gone by without you but that wouldn't be true. And I don't want to lie. Not to you.

Instead I would say that it's not easier to accept your death and it's nowhere remotely near easy to bring myself to smile over that fact, but it has at least gotten easier to prevent myself from thinking about it as much.

The less I think of it, the less it hurts I guess.

I don't know if that's strictly speaking true.

I am hardly a professional.

And even the professionals don't know either.

I'm just taking each day as it comes and wishing that all of this pain would go away to at least make life a little easier to bear. But that's never going to happen. Not if at this point it's still this bad for me.

In fact all I seem to be good for these days is looking after Jo. I can barely even bring myself to do a good job at work anymore. But then again, I do own the place. I define what a good job is in some way when you think about it.

Speaking of Jo though, she just turned seven as you might have guessed.

It was just a handful of months ago in fact.

She's even bigger than before. And so smart.

Funny even. She's got your sense of humour.

But more than that, she's got your good looks.

I wouldn't be surprised if she grows up to look just like you one of these days. Maybe that will be the day when my heart finally shatters apart again. I don't know yet.

She's moving up in school as you would expect.

Getting good grades and staying consistently at the top her class.

It's all as you would expect from a competitive soul like her.

You should see her try and play tennis with me in the court. She gets so frustrated by how good I am at the game that she pushes herself harder and harder to do better.

I go as easy on her as I can but she's getting good at it. Quickly.

I might have a word with the school to see if she can get on their team as soon as she's old enough to qualify. If she keeps her practice up with me at home, she'll be the best player they have in no time.

Actually, if she keeps up her grades and her sport, she might even be the most accomplished girl at the school by the time that she graduates. It wouldn't surprise me if she gets to do that early either.

She's so obviously talented that I swear she's being held back to keep her at the same pace as everyone else. The amount of times she tells me that she barely had to do any work in class has me convinced of that fact.

And since she's been doing so well regardless of whether or not she's being held back, I'll be rewarding her for that soon. I think a trip to that little spot near Niagara Falls should be a fitting gift given that she's wanted to see it for about a year by now.

I'll have to get her a passport obviously. As soon as I figure out where I managed to stow away her birth certificate that is.

As it happens, she asked me what her name was short for earlier, since we'd only ever called her Jo that was all she knew herself as. So I had to think for a second.

I was so sure that is was Josephine that I almost answered with it but then I remembered what we had actually agreed on the day she popped out.

We were so set on using Jo as her name that we were certain that had to stay the same but since Josephine sounded far too formal, we wrote down Joanne on the certificate. Didn't we?

I suppose I'll find out soon enough when I find it.

She'll be so happy to see the Falls as well. I know she will.

We went once didn't we? One of our earliest trips out of the country together if I recall.

I loved my time with you back then. All of it.

I can't think of a single bad moment throughout our relationship. I loved it all. It was all perfect as far as I was concerned. And it still is.

On the subject of love though, Jo asked me what the word meant recently. And I have to say that was a surprise.

For a seven year old to ask such things was well above her expected questions for someone her age but it was also a very difficult thing to put into words.

I told her that she wasn't ready to hear it and probably wouldn't understand even if she did and then changed the topic to ice-cream after that. But it did get me thinking.

What is love?

Do you know?

After my time with you I'm sure that I do but I'm not sure that I can explain it.

Perhaps I'll get around to that eventually as well.

I don't know when though. I've been busy.

As for now though Rose, I would like to propose a toast to you, wherever you are.

To the memory of you and the time we spent together.

The happiest days of my life.

Were spent with you.

My dearest Rose.

11

Dearest Rose

My world is completely falling apart around me at this stage now. It's not getting any better like everyone and their books all said and it isn't going to. It's just spiralling out of control for me now and I don't think that I can stop it anymore. I don't know how.

All those pieces that were left in the wake of your death, all those shattered remnants of the path of life that we had tirelessly forged together that were torn from my world when you passed, they were beginning to come back together for the first time since they fell. But now all of that has been thrown away. And I don't know what to do.

It's been ten years, six months, two days and fourteen hours since you died. I can remember it explicitly even now. Distinctly. I can't even seem to forget a single detail about it all. As though it were so fresh in my mind instead of the old wound that should have healed by now that it was supposed to be.

Because it still lingers. It still stings.

I remember when you first told me of your family's curse. The illness that resided in all female decedents of a long forgotten ancestor in your bloodline. The one that would lay dormant in your blood for your entire life if you would let it but the one that would awaken and thrive on your suffering should you ever conceive a child.

It sounded like something out of a horror story then. Some backstory to a character in fiction. Not something that could have happened in real life. Not something that could have happened to me. To us.

I think I even laughed a little at the time. No I actually remember it now that I think harder. And for that I am sorry my love. It was no laughing matter. You deserved more respect from me. More compassion and understanding.

You were telling me your biggest secret. The one thing that you would never tell another. The one thing that could ever stop you from finding true love in your life. And you chose to share it with me. And then I laughed.

I guess that means that was the moment when you had chosen. When you had decided what you were going to do with the rest of your life.

By telling me that story, by warning me of what future awaited you should you ever decide to have a child, you were accepting that I was the one and only man for you.

You were, securing your future.

Opening the long closed doors to your heart and allowing me in without condition. Allowing me the chance to also decide. To then two months later, be sure of what I was about to do and pop the question to you over that candlelit dinner.

You were literally handing me your heart that day. You must have been scared. And I laughed at it in return.

How you could have possibly still been happy with being by my side after that moment I do not know. But I'm glad that you chose to stay. I would have never known what I was missing had I never fallen in love with you.

Even for all of this pain caused by loving and then losing you, not knowing you at all would have still been worse for me.

By a lot.

And after you told me that it was no joke with your eyes and body language alone, slowly backing into your somewhat shallow shell in fear that I would never believe you, I accepted the truth and your eventual fate without any hesitation.

I accepted, that the price for being with you would either be that I would never become a father or that I would never get to grow old with my wife.

I couldn't do both.

And I truly wish that I could have.

I would have given anything.

Hell, if I could have surrendered my soul, heart and mind just for one more year with you, no just one more day, I would have done it gladly. I would do it again in a heartbeat had I anything else left to give after the fact.

I with that I could have done more to save you then.

That I could have found some way to cure you.

But it was too late.

I was trembling throughout the entire pregnancy. Fearful that one day you would come back from your specialist check-ups to tell me that the disease had started to spread. And even after our daughter was born and we got to take her home, that fear remained.

Because after we both welcomed our darling Jo into the world and they gave you a full hysterectomy just on the off chance that it would raise your chances of survival, I knew that the risk wouldn't completely go away.

In fact it was even higher.

I still don't understand fully how this disease works. I'm not sure that any of the doctors did either. There aren't even one hundred confirmed cases in recorded history. But I do know that it is fatal and it is genetic.

There is no cure. Or at least there wasn't at the time of your death. And there is no way to stop its spread. You can't even slow it down.

Tumours took over your body and your blood began to clot uncontrollably. Your nerves began firing on their own creating unimaginable phantom pains and your heart would often flutter and spasm every few days for hours on end.

It was a truly diabolical illness. And once it starts, there is nothing that can be done to ease it. You just suffer. And your loved ones are forced to watch as they helplessly stand to one side whilst you endure all of that alone. Unable to approach you or help you. Because there is nothing that can be done. And I wish that there was.

No amount of surgeries and no amount of pain killers could save you. All they did was needlessly give us hope that they could prevent the inevitable. And whilst you put on a brave face through it all, I knew deep down that you had resigned yourself to the fate laid down before you.

You had known for a very long time back then, that by choosing to have a child, you were also deciding that you were prepared to pay the price, to make the sacrifice, in order to bring it into the world.

But even during all of this. All of this pain. You still awoke after every procedure or harrowing night of pain with a smile on your face and a look of strength in your watered and withered eyes.

You awoke each day, ready to feed our daughter. To hold her. To kiss her and to sing to her. Each and every day. Like perfectly timed and consistent clockwork.

Or at least you did all of that, until it reached the final stages.

You did your best to be a mother to your daughter and my

god you were the best mother you could have been given the circumstances but when the final weeks of your life approached, when the disease got too challenging to control at home, you become bedridden and your time with your daughter was limited to the absurd visiting hours of that damned hospital.

You were given a few measly months of happiness with your daughter before it began and then you put yourself through what I can only describe as unimaginable torment in order to spend what few more weeks you could by her side once it started.

I am so proud of you for that.

You sacrificed so much for Jo. Didn't you?

Not only your life and your time with her but also your comfort. Just so that she might spend a few more hours with her mother holding her in her arms.

It would have been truly inspirational to watch, had it not been for the truth behind it all.

Because no matter how hard you tried to wear the brave face, we both knew that there was no coming back from this. No salvation.

It is a cruel thing, to have to give your life for your child. Especially when that child with grow up never truly know her mother because of that very sacrifice.

I wish that there could have been another way. I really do. But I respect your decision and whilst I regret that it cost you your life and me a devoted wife, I do not regret that we got a daughter out of it all.

A smiling, bouncy bundle of joy.

That is all she has ever been.

But she turned eleven just this month.

And her present, the one thing in the world that she had

wanted for years but that I had never given her, was the one thing that might well have driven a wedge between us too deeply to ever bring us back together now.

Shattering my world once again as a result.

Ever since I started telling her about you Rose, a constant question had been on her mind.

Why weren't you here?

As the years have gone on, the answer of telling her that you were simply dead began to start being too little a response. She wanted more. Much more.

She wanted to know how you had died. Where you were buried. Why I hadn't been able to save you.

And on her birthday just three days ago, I told her the truth.

I explained that you contracted a disease when she was conceived. I explained that your mother and her mother had had the same thing. That it ran in the family. And I told her that it was because we wanted a child, that you died.

She did not like hearing that.

For the first time in my life, I saw her cry after saying all of that.

And I really mean cry.

A deep sense of emotional torment, more than just pain, that brought her to screams and constant tears. And it hasn't stopped since.

She hasn't been to school, she has hardly eaten and she's refused to see me ever since. She's just locked in her room. Ignoring me out of anger. The staff can't even bring her around.

I really don't know what to do to fix this.

I fear that I've made a mistake by telling her Rose.

I had thought that by now she would be ready. But I guess not.

I am terrified now, more so than I have been in a long time, that what I have now done will be the hatchet of war between us that will never get buried. Because now that she knows, she blames both myself and her own existence for your death. Something that whilst I understand I assure her isn't true whenever I get the chance to get a word in with her.

But the root of all of this sadness is that she blames herself, for robbing her childhood of a mother.

And I don't know how to fix it.

I'm scared.

I admit it.

I am scared of losing her.

I can't go through that. Not after losing you.

I am going to have to find some way to make this up to her. And to you. But as of this moment in time, I don't know how. I'm completely clueless.

I am no doctor, no soother of the mind. What can I do?

All that I have thought about to try and resolve this, is to show her your grave.

She's never been before. I didn't think it right until she understood the significance and learned to respect the site.

But if she's this upset by learning how you died then I guess that means she's capable of processing what death is now. How final it is. So perhaps now of all times, would be the best time to show it to her.

And even if she doesn't want to go.

I'll drag her there if I have to.

I am guilty of one more thing though.

I myself haven't been to visit in a while as well.

Not in over a year now.

I suppose that since this visit with Jo will be longer than any of my own, then I should make it special. Perhaps I should finally take you all of these letters and bury them in the dirt above you so that they'll be safe. So that they'll make their way to you one way or another at long last.

And obviously that means that I'll be including this one.

Which means that I have no idea as to when if ever, you will get any more of these letters from me. I don't even know if I have what it takes to continue writing them now.

My life if boring even for me. How can I honestly keep telling you all about it if I myself don't care?

But it's about time that I gave all of the letters I have to you anyway. They're meant for your eyes only. There no good to me or my bookshelf if I keep them here.

And should this end up being the final letter that you do ever receive from me, let me say this.

I am so sorry that our time was cut so short Rose. I truly am.

I am sorry that I couldn't stay by your side forever as we had so often planned. And I am sorry, that we never got that final goodbye. I really wish we had been given the chance.

I am sorry for not writing to you more.

For not doing it every day.

And I am sorry for the pain that I have so recently caused our daughter. No father should be responsible for such a thing. I feel as though I have failed in that regard.

And I will try to do better.

To live on in your memory as the loving husband that I used to be in your eyes and to ensure that neither myself nor Jo ever forgets you.

And finally.

I promise to always love you Rose.

I promise to leave a light on for when you get home.

I promise to leave the key under the gnome on the front lawn.

And I promise to keep a fresh glass of wine on the table each night just in case.

Because from now until forever.

I will never leave your side.

Not fully.

And I sear it on my own life and soul. That my love will never fade.

I will love you until I die in this life.

And then again in whatever next life awaits me in the end.

Because you are and have always been-

My Dearest Rose.

P.S. The green gnome of course. It was your favourite.

LETTER

??

Rose

Forever ago now, I asked you a question that was very important to us both. By candlelit food and a most fitting and atmospheric setting that was in reality our tiny little dining room. The sweet aroma of lavender and sage in the air, the silent music of our eyes and hearts dancing across the divide that was the table between us. The succulent medium rare steak on that table. The bottle of half-drunk fifty year old red wine from your father's collection. The silverware. The pristine white marble plates that you had inherited from your grandfather. And the lilac tablecloth beneath it all.

Everything was perfect that night wasn't it just?

Paul McCartney singing in the distance as your Beatles album spun at a steady pace on your old record player and the snow gently settling on the cool winter's eve ground outside whilst the evening sun continued to set into velvet skies.

What more could we have asked for on such a momentous occasion? What more could we have desired to have described that evening as our ideal picture of an actual heaven to us both?

The way that dress of yours drew attention to your figure father than your bosom as many others would have and the way that your fur topped coat rested on the back of your chair like a cushion for your shoulders. It would have made you stand out against any crowd.

Your brushed straight hair. Your extended eyelashes, your plucked eye brows, your lush red lips courtesy of your favourite lipstick, and your mesmerising big brown eyes that stared deeply into my soul whenever I glanced over to them. Outlined only by your natural hue and the slightest hint of eyeliner around them.

You were the perfection that night Rose. Not the night itself.

No amount of preparation or cleaning of my old suit. No amount of forethought on how I would set the room to allow the candles and plates not to detract from the overarching presence of the rest of the table. And no amount of my cooking, however suitable it might have been for a five star restaurant as you once said, could have possibly taken away from the amazing and unforgettable sight that was you that night.

Your four inch heels, deep red and befitting of your matching dress as they might have been, did nothing to distract me from your flushed red cheeks as you sat in anticipation and embarrassment of the event to come.

The soft complexion of your skin that had never needed the aid of makeup to make attractive to myself or any other. Free of blemishes or marks of any kind like a blank canvas, just waiting to be painted.

But unlike a canvas, you didn't need painting. You were already a picture.

And you were perfect.

I will never forget how beautiful you were that night. How greatly you managed to outclass me by looks alone. How high you had set your unreachable pedestal on which you stood proud above all other competitors for my heart and affection.

I will never forget any of it.

I will remember it all.

As I suspect you too will remember how I appeared that night.

Freshly shaved and lightly dashed with cologne. Tightly strapped into my old suit that I hadn't worn since my failed job interview three years prior to starting my own company that spring and eventually buying the one that had turned me down some time later. Wearing neatly polished black shoes, a red tie that complimented your own attire and my foster father's cufflinks.

I looked like a tramp compared to the royalty sat before me.

But I guess then that this would make it just like the story. Would it not? The Lady and the Tramp? I believe that was the name. And I believe it fit that scene flawlessly. Because that was how we would have appeared to any other onlooker that night.

Myself sat there guzzling down the wine in accordance with my meal as I tried to work up my courage and you just smirking at me the whole time. Well aware of what was to come based on how much I was spoiling you alone but trying your hardest to hide it as you laughed at how hard I was still trying to impress you even though I already had.

But I didn't need to go that far in the end did I?

I had never needed to impress you. Not at any point in my life in fact.

I still don't understand how you could have ever convinced not only yourself but your parents as well that I was good enough for you. I mean, back then I was nothing. It was only after our marriage that my fame and wealth took off. So you never chose me out of stature or power did you?

Never for money?

You chose me for me. That was what I believe at least.

There's no other explanation is there?

I had nothing then any everything now.

You couldn't have seen that coming.

I had no good looks, no real charm to my personality and no humour to offer you.

I could barely even afford the home that I was living in at the time.

So whatever it was that made you stay with me all of the years prior to that moment and all of the years that followed, I am thankful for it. Because without it I would have never met you. And without it, you would have never said that one crucial word.

You remember my routine that evening don't you?

How I placed my hand into my left jacket pocket and you got all excited. Only to then pull out a slip of paper and then put on my glasses as I read it out word for word.

"To find that which you seek, look onto yourself." I explained.

You were completely dumbfounded as I recall. Having no idea what I was talking about.

Completely caught off guard.

But it didn't take you long to figure it out did it?

"Look onto yourself."

Those were the words.

And what did you find in the centre of the table between the candles, amidst the glass vase of red roses between the two of us? You found a note.

It had been sitting there the whole time. Carefully buried down so that you wouldn't be able to spot it until I had drawn your attention to it. And on this note it read.

"For a lifetime of heartache, turn me down. For an eternity of happiness, lift me up."

I remember you reading that out explicitly.

And when you did it, raising the note towards the void of darkness on the ceiling, that was when you finally spotted it. And your face changed to such shock and amazement, such joy, that my heart skipped a beat yet again.

Because up there, hanging from the pull chain that would turn on the ceiling fan and light, was a box. A deep navy blue box made of felt. One of distinct shape and design that you recognised instantly.

You stood up to grab it, pulled it down gently and opened it with such impatience that you barely even gave me a chance to get down on one knee in the meantime.

But I got there and as you stared at the large rock on the end of that polished platinum ring, you finally noticed me below you in the background. As I looked towards you with puppy dog eyes and my heart held out on a wire. Ready to fall at any moment if your next words did not help to catch it.

"I cannot think of a better way to spend the rest of my life except with you stood by my side. But not just as my best friend, and not just as my endearing girlfriend. Right here and right now, I ask of you Rose.

Will you take this hand that I extend out to you now? Until the world falls apart around us both?

Will you be mine in heart, body and soul? From now until always?

Will you marry me, my dearest Rose?"

Without hesitation I remember seeing you hand move out towards mine, gripping it so softly that I could have even mistaken you for the brisk morning wind had it not been for my eyes. And as I rose back up to your head height, being drawn in by your enticing lips and your perfect eyes until both our faces were but an inch from one another. I heard you answer.

I felt it.

"Yes!" You cried, weeping as I pulled in even closer to press my lips to yours and seal our new bond with a most passionate kiss. A kiss that lasted an eternity as I was held in your arms and you in mine.

When I pulled back, when we both calmed our nerves as your excitement grew and my body began to shake now that the fear of your saying no had passed and was replaced with the terror that such fear had been hiding, I recall that you spoke again.

And what you said to me was so like you that I don't think there was ever a time when you sounded more like the woman I know.

"You're far too smart for your own good you know. The meal was enough. You could have proposed an hour ago and it wouldn't have changed anything."

We smiled, you handed me back the ring and I slowly placed it on your finger.

I can remember feeling so accomplished then.

Like a fishermen staring at his latest catch.

Because that was what I had done Rose.

I had found the rarest fish in all the oceans of the world and I had caught her. And now that my mark was laid prominently on her finger, I was never going to let her go.

I was sure of it.

And nothing in this world or the next will ever change the way I feel about you.

My dearest Rose.

END

38081057R00070

Printed in Poland
by Amazon Fulfillment
Poland Sp. z o.o., Wrocław